Meher Pestonji is the author of two novels, *Mixed Marriage and Other Parsi Stories* and *Pervez: A Novel*, and a play, *Piano for Sale*. She has campaigned extensively for a change in rape laws, housing rights for slum-dwellers, and a more sensitive understanding of street children and their special needs.

Meher Pestonji lives in Bombay.

SADAK CHHAAP

MEHER PESTONJI

PENGUIN BOOKS

PENGUIN BOOKS
Published by the Penguin Group
Penguin Books India Pvt. Ltd, 11 Community Centre, Panchsheel Park, New
Delhi 110 017, India
Penguin Group (USA) Inc., 375 Hudson Street, New York, NY 10014, USA
Penguin Group (Canada), 90 Eglinton Avenue East, Suite 700, Toronto,
Ontario, M4P 2Y3, Canada (a division of Pearson Penguin Canada Inc.)
Penguin Books Ltd, 80 Strand, London WC2R 0RL, England
Penguin Ireland, 25 St Stephen's Green, Dublin 2, Ireland (a division of
Penguin Books Ltd)
Penguin Group (Australia), 250 Camberwell Road, Camberwell, Victoria 3124,
Australia (a division of Pearson Australia Group Pty Ltd)
Penguin Group (NZ), cnr Airborne and Rosedale Roads, Albany, Auckland
1310, New Zealand (a division of Pearson New Zealand Ltd)
Penguin Group (South Africa) (Pty) Ltd, 24 Sturdee Avenue, Rosebank,
Johannesburg 2196, South Africa

Penguin Books Ltd, Registered Offices: 80 Strand, London WC2R 0RL,
England

First published by Penguin Books India 2005
Copyright © Meher Pestonji 2005

All rights reserved
10 9 8 7 6 5 4 3 2 1

This is a work of fiction. Names, characters, places and incidents are either
the product of the author's imagination or are used fictitiously, and any
resemblance to actual persons, living or dead, events or locales is entirely
coincidental.

Typeset in Sabon by InoSoft Systems, Noida
Printed at Baba Barkhanath Printers, New Delhi

For Shafique, Abdul, Santosh, Vishal, Rasool,
and others lost
in the currents of life.

And for all those
who try to create cross-currents.

After you're born
you cannot fit back
into Mother's womb

You have no choice
but to bump, bruise, bleed
and still crawl on and on

One day you stand
then walk
then run

Now when you fall
you can always
break a bone.

He could have sworn the newspaper package moved. Not a gentle flapping in the breeze. Not the rustle of paper crinkling into different forms. Another kind of movement, from within.

Rahul had been observing the oblong parcel for a while. It sat on a bench at the deserted end of the railway platform as he sat on another, sucking a mango. He had been keeping an eye on it, waiting for someone to claim it, waiting to finish his mango before running off with his find.

Rahul could run fast, faster than any other station boy. The mango was one of his prizes for speed. He had run off with it from Karim-bhai's stall while the fruit vendor was attending to a client. Karim-bhai had shouted but he couldn't leave a customer haggling over a basket of mangoes to chase a kid flicking just one. Rahul would get a whack later, but he was used to that. If he thought up a fresh story about tough life in the village, Karim-bhai would melt. If the day's business had been good, he might even get another mango, gratis.

Not all station vendors were kind. Hamid thrashed him when he saw Rahul wearing a shirt missing from his stall. Heera-bai had flung scalding oil at him as he ran off with a handful of vadas from the freshly fried pile for sale. His legs ensured he didn't get caught. Speed was his greatest asset.

Once in a while his nimble fingers picked a pocket. And once in a while he would strike the jackpot. Like the time a wallet contained fifteen five-hundred-rupee notes. He had never seen so much money. He couldn't count how much but he knew it was a lot. Back home, a fortune, even in Bombay it was enough to make him important as long as it lasted.

He planned to see seven films, starting with *Devdas*, and to wear new clothes every day. He chose a shirt from Hamid's stall and handed him a five-hundred-rupee note with panache. How triumphant he felt as Hamid's eyeballs rolled at the sight of the pale yellow currency note. '*Chutiya*, just ten years old and become a pocket-maar already!' snarled Hamid, taking the shirt back from Rahul.

'No, yaar. I found a wallet on the tracks.'

'*Sala badmash*. You want this shirt, pay hundred rupees.'

'But just now you were shouting forty rupees, forty rupees . . .'

'That's for honest customers. How many shirts have you stolen from me already?'

'I'll buy my shirt somewhere else!' cried Rahul edging away.

Hamid's fist closed over the five-hundred-rupee note. 'You're not getting this back,' he snarled. 'Don't act tough or I'll tell that cop you're carrying stolen money.'

The newspaper parcel would not contain money. Of that Rahul was certain. Maybe it would contain clothes, or something he could sell. What if it contained a blanket? Something to cover him from head to toe, giving warmth, protecting from mosquitoes, cutting off the glare of neon.

He sucked hard at the mango seed, juice dribbling down his elbows, thinking how nice it would be to have a blanket. That's when the parcel changed shape.

Was it a food parcel then? Had rats got to it already?

All the flesh was off the mango seed now. Fibres fringed its oval shape, long on one side, hugging close on the other. Rahul examined the colourless seed with satisfaction, giving it one last suck before tossing it onto the tracks. Then he got up, licking his hands. Nonchalantly he strolled over to the bench, scanning directions. Still no claimant. But another distinct movement. Must be rotting food attacked by rats, he thought, losing interest.

Out of curiosity he parted the paper, and recoiled, mouth agape, horror hitting his face. For a few seconds he stood transfixed, eyes glued to the parcel. Then he backed off, turned, and started running, faster than he had ever run, though no one was chasing him. He ran barefoot the entire length of the platform, past the tea stall and juice stall and snacks counter, past Chhotu the cobbler, past the ticket collector, past three hijras clapping for alms, and didn't stop running even when he reached the street. Blindly he ran past fruit and flower sellers, pushing past shoppers as he shot across the road, oblivious of a taxi driver's abuse. He flung open a door in a grey wall under the flyover and looked wildly from face to face, panting. Then he grabbed Aparna's arm and cried, 'Didi! Didi! Come with me, didi!'

Aparna ignored Rahul. She continued talking on the phone as he tugged impatiently at her dupatta. 'Where? Near Capitol cinema . . . No, don't try to shift him,' she said calmly. 'St George's is the nearest hospital. Our volunteer will reach in half an hour.' She put down the phone and turned to Victor who was piling mattresses in a corner of the drab room. 'A child is vomiting blood on the pavement near Capitol. Send someone to take him to hospital.'

'Didi, come fast,' cried Rahul, pulling the dupatta off her shoulders.

She smacked him lightly on the wrist. 'What's the matter now, Rahul? Is a cop chasing you or a goonda?'

'*Koi nahin*! Someone has forgotten a baby on the platform.'

'What!'

'At the end of platform number three. Wrapped in newspaper. Big-big ants are on the baby's face.' He was close to tears.

Aparna knew that for once Rahul wasn't lying. Handing over Sharan's helpline to Victor she barked instructions before hurrying out with Rahul, calling Shekhar to follow. Past the colourful fruit and flower market and into the station, past passengers, beggars and vendors, past stinking toilets to the far end where the package was still on the bench.

'You poor thing,' murmured Aparna, her heart wrenching. 'Go fetch a policeman, we have to lodge an FIR,' she instructed Shekhar. He sped off. Gently, she started plucking ants off the baby's face. The baby stayed still, barely able to whimper. Its red dress was of flimsy material, an old sari or dupatta. Black kajal on the left cheek was its sole protection against evil spirits.

'Did you see who left the baby here?' she asked. Rahul shook his head. 'Someone . . . a woman . . . nearby . . .?'

'No, didi. I was eating a mango on this bench. I looked at the parcel for five-ten minutes.' He fidgeted uncomfortably, reluctant to reveal his intentions.

'How can anyone abandon a child,' sighed Aparna, wiping the baby's cheek with her dupatta, its edge turned black with the kajal. The baby screwed up its face, but before Aparna could pick it up Shekhar appeared with a disdainful-looking constable.

'Must be a girl,' the constable said. 'Second case this month. Happens in Ganapati festival. Parents think some good person will take it home to earn *punya*.' Reluctantly he took out a lathi from his leather belt and flicked open the newspaper.

A cry escaped the child's lips. Aparna gasped. Rahul's eyes widened into round marbles.

'It's been burnt,' muttered the policeman, peering at the little legs covered with angry red blisters. 'I told you it would be a girl. They wanted to get rid of her.'

'We have to get her to hospital,' cried Aparna.

'Let the poor creature die in peace,' advised the cop.

Aparna swung on him like a tigress. 'We are going to take her to hospital and you are going to file a case of attempted murder against whoever did this to her.'

'How to find parents from thousands in the station? Forget you found the child. In a few hours she'll be dead. I'll report unidentified body found at station. Case open and shut same day.'

'And you'll be fired from your job the same day!' blazed Aparna. 'Show me your buckle number. The commissioner is my mother's brother.'

The cop's attitude changed. 'Sorry, memsa'ab . . . I'll file FIR like you say . . .'

'Shekhar, go with him. Make sure he writes the FIR correctly. Don't sign anything till I come. I'm taking the baby to hospital. Rahul, come with me.'

Rahul watched Aparna take off her dupatta, fold it into a rectangle, lift the baby off the soiled newspaper and wrap her up. The movement chafed the blistered legs and the whimpering increased. Gently, Aparna settled it into the crook of her arm. The baby sighed and fell silent again.

He didn't want to see the baby die, so he sat on the front seat next to the cab driver. They didn't speak on the short drive to the hospital. Every few minutes he heard Aparna urging the driver to go faster, avoid potholes, not brake so hard. Then they were in the emergency ward, Aparna unfolding the swaddles on a white Formica table, telling a bespectacled doctor how and where the baby had been found. In the middle of examining the child the doctor noticed Rahul, grubby, dishevelled, but apparently with Aparna.

'Who's he?'

'He's the boy who found her.'

'Sure he didn't steal her?'

'Why would he do that?'

The doctor shrugged. 'Urchins will steal anything.'

'Your job is to treat the baby, not cast aspersions on a child!' flared Aparna.

Reluctantly the doctor turned back to the baby. 'She will need antibiotic injections, a saline drip . . . I don't know if we can save her but her only hope is if we put her into the neonatal ICU. That'll be expensive.'

'Our NGO will bear the cost,' replied Aparna.

He looked at her quizzically. 'Are you sure you want to get into this? You've done your duty. Let nature take its course.'

Aparna drew a deep breath. 'Man, not nature, burnt this child. We must give her a chance.'

The doctor raised his eyebrows but Aparna stayed firm. At last he started giving instructions to a nurse. The baby was carried away.

'Normally we don't admit to the ICU without a deposit but I've authorized an exception,' he told Aparna. 'Pay the deposit tomorrow. Medicines will have to be bought from the chemist down the road. Also intravenous drips. If you have to go somewhere, leave someone to run up and down. First fill up these forms.' He thrust a sheaf of papers at Aparna and strode down the corridor.

She stared thoughtfully after his receding figure, then led Rahul to a red plastic chair. 'Come, Rahul,' she said more cheerily than she felt. 'Let's give the baby a name. What would you like to name her?'

He was taken aback at this unexpected privilege. Recovering fast, he looked skyward, placing a finger impishly against the corner of his mouth. 'Rani? Or Kajol?' he speculated, rolling his eyes.

'Why Rani or Kajol?' asked Aparna, bemused.

'Haven't you seen *Kuch Kuch Hota Hai*?'

She laughed. 'You want to name her after a film star!'

'Why not!' His finger went back on his mouth as he screwed up his face, thinking. 'Raja-Rani? But Kajol was so kind to children in the film . . .'

'Let's call her Kajol.'

He said 'okay', shaking his body approvingly from side to side. Aparna wrote 'Kajol' with a flourish on the form. 'Next is her father's name. What shall we call him?'

'Rahul,' he said without hesitation.

Aparna burst into laughter and tousled the youngster's

hair. 'Want to be a father already?'

'I found her, didi,' he said shyly.

'So you did. Okay, we'll put her father's name as Rahul. And for the surname shall we say Stationwallah?'

Rahul nodded, grinning from ear to ear.

For the next three hours he sat on a wooden bench outside the ICU, the only bedraggled boy among relatives with anxious faces. Twice the nurse came out to hand him prescriptions. He ran to the chemist with whom Aparna had made an arrangement for late payment and ran back, face flushed.

'Who's your patient?' asked an elderly gentleman who sat beside Rahul.

'Small baby.'

'Your sister?'

'No. I . . . I found her.'

'Found her?'

'Someone left her at the station in a newspaper.'

'And you brought her to hospital?'

'No-no. Aparna-didi brought her. I came with didi.'

Rahul turned away from the man's curious gaze. Normally, well-dressed gentlemen avoided street kids like him. The nurse beckoned, cutting short the conversation. He had to run to the chemist for an injection. This time the chemist shook his head: it was not in stock. Rahul could get it from the chemist down the road, but he had no money. His chest constricted in an unfamiliar way. The baby hovered between life and death. She needed an injection. Her life depended on him.

He picked up the receiver of a public telephone and dialled the toll-free number, 1098. Victor had left to pick up the sick child from Capitol. Shekhar was at the police station with Aparna. He didn't want to ask Salim what he should do. Salim was one of Sharan's bullies. Despondently he trooped back to the ICU and told the nurse that the injection was unavailable.

'Go to another chemist, boy. The baby's gasping. She may not last long.'

'I don't have money,' mumbled Rahul. 'I don't know when didi will return.'

The gentleman he had been talking to earlier intervened. 'How much does the injection cost?' he asked the nurse.

'About three hundred.'

Taking out his wallet he handed Rahul three green notes. 'My wife's treatment is costing three thousand per day. We'll be happy to help an unfortunate child.'

Rahul sped away. When he returned, the gentleman was waiting with a Cadbury's bar. 'You're a good boy,' he said, handing it to Rahul. Rahul was confused. No one had ever called him a good boy. No one had gifted him a chocolate.

He spent the night on the bench where he had found the baby. He reached there after the station population had settled into their niches for the night. His favourite bench between the bookstall and Ramu's tea stall had an overladen trolley in front of it. He could have gone to Sharan but his legs carried him to the bench.

The soiled newspaper, crumpled into a ball, lay under a lamp post without light, a lighter grey than the surrounding darkness. The same paper whose flapping had drawn his attention to the baby. He stared at it, holding his chin in his palms. Stretching a leg he pulled the paper towards him, smoothed it straight, folded it into a rectangle. Placing the folded paper under his head he stared at the sky. No clouds. And the stars were barely visible. But his old friend the moon was in its watermelon avatar: two pointed tips and a curved centre, poised at a cheeky angle. Rahul felt comfortable with the moon. It had accompanied him from his village to bus and train, past unknown towns and cities all the way to Bombay, a name he had only heard on the black-and-white *gram panchayat* TV set. Long, long ago.

The baby made him think of his mother. Thoughts banished for months. She must have cried when he left, but not for long. The contractor would have seen to that. And his sisters had to be fed. Had she forgotten him after three years? Relieved to be rid of him, like the baby's mother? That was not a pleasant thought. The moon, he knew, would never abandon him.

Rahul curled into a foetal position and stared at the moon. The makeshift pillow emitted a faint odour. His eyes remained fixed on the moon till his eyelids drooped and he breathed in the steady rhythm of a child asleep.

'I became a father yesterday,' he told Karim-bhai the next day.

'*Arre!* His worm can't become a stick yet and he's all set to become a father!' chuckled the middle-aged vendor, affectionately slapping Rahul. 'Tell me who the girl is and I'll do the job for you.'

'No girl.'

'No girl? You are an *ullu*, what? Men become men without becoming fathers. What's the use of becoming a father without a girl?'

He caught Rahul's wrist and took him behind the fruit stall. He plucked a banana from a bunch. Laughing, he pulled down Rahul's shorts. 'When your *popat* grows as big as this, think of becoming a father. *Ja bachcha, kela kha*. You'll have enough problems without fathering a child.'

'Just listen to my story,' insisted Rahul.

'Another one? With more *mirch-masala* than the last, I bet!'

But at Sharan he was the day's hero. Early that morning he had been surprised to find Bablu shaking him awake. 'Why are you here? Everybody's looking for you.'

'*Chhod* yaar. Let me sleep.'

'You've slept enough. Come on. They're making kheer.'

Rahul opened his eyes without moving. 'Kheer? It's not Sunday . . .'

'For you, yaar!'

'For me?' All traces of sleep vanished.

'You saved a child yesterday. Don't you remember?'

A slow smile spread over Rahul's face as the previous day's events flooded his mind. 'So . . . they're making kheer,' he said, unfolding his limbs. The newspaper fluttered off the bench. 'Will I get double share?' he asked as he bent to retrieve it.

'You'll get five shares if you want. Victor and Anand aren't giving anyone till you come.'

They weaved their way through the rush-hour crowd, inviting glares when their grubby hands brushed a pallu or dupatta. Sunlight streaming through cracks in the corrugated ceiling gave sudden life to invisible dust specks swirling into rays. One ray reflected a dupatta's orange onto Rahul's face, another shifted it to red. Ignoring the kaleidoscope on his body-screen, Rahul made his way to the kheer.

'*Aya!* Hero *aya!*' whooped the boys as they surrounded a grinning Rahul. Amidst hugging and back-slapping he was carried into Sharan where a steaming bowl of sweet kheer was thrust into his hands. A cheer went up as he took the first sip. Then the boys abandoned him, rushing for their own plates. And the questions flowed. How did he find the baby? Were her legs badly burnt? Did the policeman really want her to die? Did he really give his name as her father?

The bench became the focus of attention. Throughout the day boys visited it in awe as Rahul sharpened his narrative skills, describing the pathetic parcel with the baby inside, the ogre of a policeman who looked like the devil, the doctor with spiral horns popping out of his ears. And Rahul himself in command, like a knight in shining armour, even advising Aparna. So dramatic was his rendering that he began to believe it himself, especially when the sceptical Karim-bhai came by to give him a pat on the back.

Before he knew of Sharan, Rahul had spent his nights on the benches and floors of numerous stations and streets. A runaway from an early age, he was used to subsisting on minimums—sleeping where he could, eating leftovers, grabbing food from vendors. Escaping a poverty-stricken, turbulent home life, he had made his way to Bombay, his dream world. He had seen it on television, the tall buildings and buses bigger than houses. He had heard that no one starves in Bombay. That was enough.

Bombay had all this and more, he discovered, but no place for him. No one starved because Bombayites had much to waste. Restaurant garbage provided a feast for a child whose only treat had been wild berries, and free food was distributed daily at dargas and temples.

The problem was sleep. He was used to cold hard floors, even rats running over him and mosquitoes biting. But there was no space. Pavements and platforms were controlled by goons. To sleep, you had to belong to a gang or pay *hafta*. Rahul rarely had money. Every few hours he would be prodded with a stick or a boot and a nasty snarl would tell him to move. A night of undisturbed sleep was the one luxury he missed from his village.

Sharan filled that need. It also provided a locker to keep his two belongings—his rag-picker's sack and the tattered sheet that became his bedroll at night. But no blessing comes undiluted, and Sharan's problem was its resident bullies. Rahul had been slapped and forced to wash older boys' clothes, fetch bidis for them, massage their legs. When he got fed up of Salim's gang he would return to the station, only to scurry back when the goons became too demanding.

Aparna, a social worker, ran Sharan, with day-to-day chores being rotated among boys. Grandiose designations were the sugar-coating to work. The boy in charge was ceremoniously titled *pradhan mantri*, a prime minister, who functioned with a cabinet of an education minister, a health minister and a food minister. Victor was currently *pradhan mantri* and Shekhar was *arogya mantri*, the health minister. The designations provided status among the loosely banded community of kids.

At Sharan's next weekly meeting Bablu proposed that Rahul be appointed a *mantri* since he was now a father. The boys unanimously agreed. Rahul felt pleased. The problem was the portfolio. *Shiksha mantri* was out since he couldn't even spell his name and the popular food ministry was over-staffed. That left health.

Rahul liked working with Shekhar, the reigning health minister, a thin boy with a pockmarked face who had been trained as a *bal-daktar*. Shekhar administered first aid to the thirty-odd boys living at Sharan and another twenty who frequented it. Each morning, as Anand, the food minister, made tea, Shekhar added ginger to some chai in a smaller *dekchi* for boys with colds and coughs, then gave them amla-haldi dissolved in water to clear chest congestion. Cuts and wounds were treated with a turmeric-milk paste. Herbal remedies reduced the drain on

Sharan's resources, though Crocin, Lomotil and Combiflam were available at a pinch. Shekhar was also responsible for taking the boys who needed professional attention to hospital.

As junior health minister, Rahul's duty was to keep Sharan clean. In weekly talks with colourful slides Victor and Shekhar stressed the connection between health and hygiene as half the boys dozed off. Now Rahul listened. He had always known mosquitoes were a nuisance—those that buzzed before biting as well as those that bit silently. When he learnt that mosquitoes cause malaria and breed in stagnant water, he pointed to the choked gutter outside Sharan's window. A few months earlier Rahul had watched Bablu shiver and shake as his temperature soared to 103 degrees. He had recovered after a miserable spell at the hospital but remained feeble for weeks. After malaria Bablu lost his speed. He often got caught after their escapades. Rahul dreaded malaria, so he volunteered to clean the gutter outside Sharan. Impressed by his zeal, Shekhar proposed he be paid two rupees per day. Rahul's head swelled by two whole inches. It felt as important as having a job.

'Do you want to visit Kajol?'

The question caught Rahul by surprise. Almost a month had passed since that fateful afternoon. As the tiny ant-covered face swam into memory he nodded enthusiastically. Aparna promised to take him the next day.

He spent the evening fretting, wanting to take Kajol a gift but not wanting to start on a wrong note by filching it. He strolled between hawkers selling handkerchiefs, envelopes, agarbatti, bedsheets, pens, chappals. Nothing seemed right for a baby. He wandered into a gully lined with fresh vegetable stalls and inspected the red pyramids of tomatoes between green and white spires of cabbage and cauliflower with bunches of spinach, fenugreek and kothmir amid patches of purple brinjals. After the vegetable vendors were the fruit stalls, with sweet-limes strung into *torans*, banana bunches hanging between knots on strings and pomegranates split open and carved into zigzag points, like flower petals.

Rahul looked longingly at the apples and oranges. The fruit seller was fat but the boy beside him looked like he could run. Rahul waited till the boy was weighing apples and the fat man got busy chatting with an equally fat woman. Quietly, his fingers reached for an orange and his feet took off. He ran blindly down the lane and turned into the doorway of a dilapidated building. No one was following him. He sat on the steps and peeled the orange, slipping a piece into his mouth. Slurping the sweet-sour juice, he spat out pips and smacked his lips in pleasure.

Behind him he heard a sound. A small girl with a butterfly bow on her head was staring at the stranger on her doorstep. In her hand she held a fish-shaped squeaky toy. This was just what he wanted—Kajol would love a squeaky toy. The girl kept eyeing him. Rahul approached her and held out his hand. She extended her free hand. Clean and grubby hands clasped. Their eyes locked and they smiled. He extended his second hand with half the orange. She held out the squeaky fish. In a flash Rahul swapped the fish with the orange, and was off. In the backdrop he heard a wail.

The next morning he was dressed and waiting before Aparna arrived. She was looking pretty in a pale pink salwar-kameez with tiny pink earrings dangling from her earlobes. According to routine, she checked Childline's night calls. A sick boy had been brought to Sharan by Shekhar. The second call was from a twelve-year-old domestic servant complaining about her employers who forced her to work long hours and gave barely enough food. Advising Victor to contact her employers, Aparna picked up her bag to leave.

'Where did you get this?' she asked, eyeing the orange-yellow fish.

'I found it,' he lied.

In the taxi she told him that Kajol had been out of ICU for some time, that she had put on two kilos since they found her and had become a favourite of the nurses.

'Did the policeman find her parents?' he wanted to know.

Aparna shook her head. 'The inspector told me they have more important work. Like going after the underworld and protecting politicians. No one has registered a case of a missing child so they couldn't care less.'

Rahul stared past the speeding shops, lost in thought. Had his mother registered a case of a missing child? Had cops in his village been as callous as this one? Did Munni still remember him? To banish depression, he tried to reconstruct the features of the baby in the flimsy dress. He was anxious to see Kajol. In the month since he had stumbled upon her, his life had improved. He attributed his good fortune to her.

The first thing Rahul noticed was her long eyelashes. A curly mop framed her olive face. But her left leg was still in bandages.

'*Bahut khubsoorat hai*,' he murmured, his eyes shining. 'Give her to me.'

'You'll drop her,' cautioned Aparna, slipping one hand

under the baby's head, the other under her bottom, and lifting her out of the cot.

'I used to carry my sister!'

Aparna looked into his defiant, pleading eyes. 'Okay,' she said warily. 'Sit down. I'll put her in your lap.'

Her concern seemed excessive to a boy used to running across fields with Munni straddled across his hip. They found a bench in the corridor; Rahul sat down and placed the fish beside him. Aparna lowered Kajol and instructed him how to place his hands. She made him feel awkward. He would have liked to stroke the sleeping face, feel its softness without his hands being trapped.

Then Kajol yawned. 'Look didi! She opened her mouth!'

Aparna smiled, delighted by the progress of her protégé. 'In a few months she'll be walking and talking,' she said softly.

Kajol opened her eyes to an unfamiliar face. Her mouth contorted and she began to cry. Aparna took her from Rahul and started rocking her. She refused to calm down. Aparna looked frantically for the nurse, who seemed to have disappeared. 'She must be hungry,' she muttered, lifting Kajol to her shoulder. The baby only cried louder.

Accidentally Rahul sat on the fish. The squeak startled the baby and she stopped crying. Rahul lifted the fish to the baby's face and squeaked it. She gurgled. He squeaked it again, against her cheek. Her face broke into a smile as she wriggled in Aparna's arms. Rahul was ecstatic. He spent an hour with Kajol, returning to Sharan with tales of her beauty and his success in quieting her when Aparna had failed.

After that he pestered Aparna to take him again and again till the nurses got used to seeing him even without her.

three

———————

When Rahul first reached Bombay he had been too scared to cross the road. He had travelled thousands of miles on trains with unknown destinations, driven by the magic word 'Bombay'. Conductors ignored the ticketless beggar boy. Passengers gave their leftover food to be rid of his dirty hands and pleading eyes. He had a roof over his head, he did not go hungry, so he had no complaints.

But Bombay roads were something else. The roads he was familiar with were mostly unpaved and rarely had more than a few vehicles passing every half hour. In Bombay vehicles of varied shapes and sizes sped in different directions all at once. Any effort to weave through them was certain to crush him to a pulp. Yet they mesmerized him, enticing him to step into a bigger world.

For weeks he stood near the station's exit, too scared to venture beyond the news vendor on the pavement, staring in awe at crowds rushing around without knocking each other down, at hawkers bellowing louder than bulls, at buses large enough to house a dozen families. Each evening he would return to the security of brown-and-yellow local trains, which carried him to the last stop and back till the sun rose. Inside trains, he could sleep secure.

'You want to cross? Come, I'll take you.'

Rahul turned to face a boy twice his age and height carrying a bundle of polythene bags. He shook his head. The boy walked past, crossed the road, and disappeared into the awning of a shop. In a few minutes he reappeared without the bundle. Passing Rahul he said, 'Give me any plastics you find. With food, without food, clean, dirty, doesn't matter. Give them to me, okay?'

Rahul followed the boy beyond the platforms to a space between the tracks under the pedestrian overbridge where seven or eight boys were playing *patta*. The boy squatted among the card players, placing a coin at the centre of the circle. Another boy dealt cards. He lost. Nonchalantly, he put in another coin. Rahul stood on the side, watching.

He started collecting plastics, handing them to Salim, till one of the card players said, 'Why don't you sell your own plastic?'

The idea took root. Rahul worked out a strategy to cross the road. He would cross in the early morning before the cars, buses and trucks came on and wait till the scrap dealer opened his shop. Everything went according to plan. For five days he collected polythene bags, sleeping on top of them to prevent them flying off in the breeze. On the sixth day he sold his haul for two rupees. Exhilarated, he ran across the road in full traffic, forgetting his fears. At the card players' adda he proudly put down his coin.

'Eh-eh, where did you get money?' asked Salim.

'I sold plastic.'

'You sold plastic? You're supposed to give it to me!'

'Leave him alone. He's got to grow up,' said the boy who had initially made the suggestion.

'*Chup baith*! He's my *chela*.'

'He's just a kid. Like we were . . .' Turning to Rahul,

he added, 'Listen, boy. If anyone bothers you, tell them they have to answer Vicky.'

It was good to have a protector. Vicky showed him the corner where the canteen disgorged garbage, a better alternative to passengers' leftovers. He introduced him to a chai-wallah who gave tea in exchange for washing cups. And he taught him to be a 'seater'.

'If you can jump on to a moving train you can work for me,' Vicky told him as they walked along the platform. That was easy. Rahul ran and boarded a train streaming in.

'Good,' said Vicky, jumping in through another door. 'Now stretch across the seat. Don't move till I give the word.'

The train slowed to a halt and passengers rushed in, dumping bundles and bags to grab space. Commotion reigned till all seats were occupied. Rahul and Vicky held on. As latecomers trickled in, Vicky bargained. 'Window seat fifty, inside forty,' he called. Three passengers ignored him. Then an elderly couple entered. A bit of haggling, and the two seats were sold for sixty-five. Vicky handed Rahul twenty rupees. He was a kingpin among 'seaters', with seven boys working for him.

Rahul also learnt he could collect newspapers, magazines and Bisleri bottles from incoming trains and sell them to the scrap dealer. 'Don't sell bottles to the shop,' advised Vicky. 'Fill them with water and sell them on the next train.' That was more lucrative than the seven rupees for a kilo of bottles the scrap dealer paid. Passengers paid ten for just one. It was worth the effort of filling the bottles and resealing them over a candle flame.

He would linger over discarded glossies, gazing at the

seductive forms of Urmila, Aishwarya, Madhuri, the slick, sleek Shah Rukh Khan, the hunky Sanjay Dutt. Daily he would see films in dimly lit video parlours for one or two rupees. Melting into the darkness he would forget the grime and struggle of station existence, transported to snow-clad mountains, gardens bursting with flowers, heroines more beautiful than any woman he had seen. Invariably he would fall asleep before the film ended, prolonging his tryst with dreamland, only to be jolted awake by the inevitable nudge and a harsh voice telling him to scoot or pay for the next show.

As Vicky's protégé, Rahul had a corner of the adda to sleep in, under the naked sky. One morning he was woken with a shout. 'Come fast! A pipe's burst!' Sleepily he followed Vicky along the tracks till they came to a jet of water gushing high into the air. Half a dozen boys were dancing under the shower. Vicky stripped and ran to join them. A piece of soap appeared from nowhere. The boys scrubbed, laughed, scrambled over each other.

'For the next three days we won't smell *sadak chhaap*,' laughed Vicky as they pulled washed clothes over wet bodies.

Rahul hadn't enjoyed himself so much in ages. It was his first real bath in Bombay.

It was Vicky who took Rahul to Sharan when he saw the rash on his palm. 'I had the same rash months ago,' he told Rahul, who had scratched at his hand till the skin broke and blood leaked.

Aparna took one look and shook her head. 'This is no ordinary rash. It looks like scabies,' she said. 'Show me your other hand. See, it's starting here as well.' She called to a boy arranging bottles on a shelf. 'Shekhar, look at this hand. I think it's scabies.'

Meher Pestonji

Shekhar put away the last bottle and squinted over Rahul's hand. 'Bablu had scabies,' he murmured. 'Let's try the same treatment.'

Aparna looked sceptical. 'I don't know . . . Bablu was living here. This boy is on the streets. How will he keep clean?' She turned to Rahul with an anxious smile. 'Will you stay at Sharan till your hands heal?'

Rahul looked incredulous. He hadn't stayed in a place with a roof over his head in ages.

'Scabies is a dirt-related disease,' she continued. 'Shekhar will grind neem, tulsi and haldi into a paste and rub it all over your body. You'll have to keep it on for two-three hours. Never mind the itch. You have to keep clean, have a bath every day.'

He looked at the floor unhappily. How would he eat if he didn't go to the garbage bin? Where would he find water to bathe?

She came to his rescue as if reading his thoughts. 'At Sharan we give subsidized meals. If you don't have money you can pay later. We also have a bathroom you can use.' Rahul could hardly believe his ears.

On the first day, as he sat self-consciously, covered with Shekhar's paste, Bablu appeared out of nowhere and popped a bag in Rahul's ears, falling over with laughter when he saw the startled expression on the newcomer's face. Rahul's ego prickled more than his smarting skin. He nursed a childish desire for revenge.

As Shekhar rubbed paste on him the next day, Rahul's eyes searched for Bablu. As soon as he saw Bablu, Rahul ran into a head-on embrace, smearing Bablu with paste. 'What for?' sputtered Bablu.

'For doing "phut" in my ears yesterday.'

'I'll do "phut" again.'

'And I'll paste you again.'

Eight-year-old eyes appraised each other. Then Bablu said, 'Get rid of the paste, yaar. I'll show you best vada-pao in Dadar.'

A week later they were standing at Heera-bai's sizzling tawa waiting for freshly fried vadas. Behind her stretched the colourful flower market with mounds of puja flowers graded in orange, yellow, yellow-white and white alongside red and orange piles of champa, sontake, jacunti. Behind the flower sellers, a portrait of a multi-armed goddess, wearing a garland of mogras and tiny, red rosebuds, presided over transactions. The ground was strewn with trampled flowers.

A girl, barely older than Rahul, sat stringing roses and lilies into *torans* beside a grey-haired woman with a stall of *venis*—mogra, jagad, aboli—woven into symmetrical rounds edged with pink and orange. A hub of women hovered around, selecting *venis* and fixing them to their hair. As supply ran short she called to the girl to switch from *torans* to *venis*. Rahul watched nimble fingers weave delicate flowers. The girl had only a droopy red flower in her own hair.

Assorted flower fragrances combined with the aroma of frying vadas. Heera-bai scooped a perforated spoon into hot oil and lifted it, tapping lightly against the tawa to drain excess oil. Placing each vada between two halves of pao she handed them to the boys. Rahul bit into the vada with relish. These were tastier than the ones at the railway stall—the potato soft, batter crisp, spiced with green chillies and coriander.

Bablu was more fun than the card players. He took

Rahul to a park with swings, slides and a jungle gym. He played cricket with a pink plastic ball that refused to bounce. On trains he tapped stones like castanets, singing *Hum tum ek kamre mein bandh ho* in a high-pitched voice.

Rahul stretched out his time at Sharan till he learnt he could stay as long as he liked. When storm clouds began to gather, he advised Vicky to move in as well. It was Rahul's second monsoon in Bombay. The first had been sheer hell. He had never seen so much rain in his life. Sheets of water poured insanely out of a grey sky as sun and moon abandoned the earth to its doom. Huts along the track were covered in blue polythene sheets held down by stones. The boys tried erecting similar sheets over their adda. Without a roof to rest on, the sheet flapped loose with the first gusts of wind. Slits appeared at stretch points near strings tied to pillars. Their roof became a sieve. It was tough to remain dry for more than a few hours, impossible to find a dry corner to sleep. Rahul was lucky to find a torn cloth banner flapping on a lamp post. It was superimposed with the face of a tiger and covered him with trickles of black ink the two weeks he used it as a bedsheet. When it disintegrated, he again shivered through nights, snuggling between boys for warmth, thankful he had connected with Vicky before the dream city began to degenerate into hell.

On a day less wet than usual, an enterprising hawker spread coarse bedcovers over a plastic sheet outside the station. Commuters crowded around factory seconds, picking up bedsheets at half price, haggling. Rahul mingled with the crowd. Warily he eyed the hawker. As soon as his back was turned, Rahul grabbed a thick sheet and ran. It was his first theft. That night he slept snugly, to the envy of the others. Vicky crawled under the sheet beside him. Three days later he asked Rahul to give up his sheet, but Rahul refused.

By the next monsoon Rahul was well ensconced at Sharan. When Vicky came down with gastroenteritis he urged his friend to move in. Initially Vicky resisted, but gave in when the stomach gripes intensified, with both upper and lower orifices ejecting the contents of his bowels. He was instructed to chew neem and tulsi leaves mixed with turmeric, and sip a sugar-salt solution to minimize dehydration.

By the time he recovered, Vicky had made up his mind to move in. Aparna was quick to spot his nurturing instinct and natural sense of justice, and began grooming him for leadership.

four

___

Bare toes dug lightly into the earth as the swing carried him up and down. The chains of the second swing had been twisted and the swing rolled upside down for the night. Except for a few sleeping men, Rahul had the park to himself. But instead of climbing the jungle gym or swinging hard and fast as he usually did, he kept his swing low and slow.

Ever since he had found Kajol, Rahul had spent his nights on the station bench. Each night he would finish sweeping and swabbing at Sharan, take his bedroll, and head out, developing a proprietorial attachment to 'my bench'. Tonight it was occupied by a stranger. And that stranger was a woman. Who was she? Why had she chosen his bench? Was she Kajol's mother? What if she wanted the baby back? What if she burnt her again? Dropping his bedroll at the foot of the lamp post without light, he had wandered into the park, his head bursting with confusion. The swing would settle his thoughts. He shut his eyes and began to swing faster. Whatever happened, he wouldn't let anybody hurt Kajol again.

He bit his lip as his toes hit the earth harder and the swing carried him higher, staring up at the full face of the moon. The moon was no comfort when dark thoughts invaded his head. He stopped the swing and turned away. A silvery sky, deceptively soothing, peeped between leaves.

He saw Kajol almost every day. His eyes became moist whenever he recalled the day she had recognized him. She was in her cot, wriggling, when he arrived. The bandage on her left leg was smaller, but the leg lay limp at her side. Positioning himself at eye level he jabbed his thumbs into his ears, waggling his fingers and making clucking sounds. 'Kajol,' he called softly. Slowly the tiny face puckered, the sulky look left her mouth and her eyes lit up. Exhilarated, Rahul jumped up and down, waving elephant ears around her cot. Kajol kept gurgling.

After that her eyes lit up each time he approached and she would leap from the nurse's arms to him. For an hour he would play with her, sticking out his tongue, waggling fingers, making funny sounds. When Kajol cried because she saw him leave, Rahul's heart swelled with an emotion he could not define. Had his mother felt like this when he cried, he wondered. Why had she not intervened when that drunken man of hers slapped him? He was a no-good louse who climbed on her and made heavy noises. He spent all his money on liquor but expected to be fed. And she, who earned barely enough, had no qualms feeding him.

His mother had become a blurred memory—a frayed sari covering her head, with his sister straddled across her hip and a *ghamela* of bricks or sand on her head, walking very straight, hips swaying. Some days he accompanied them to the construction site. Some days he would mind the hut, where rice or wheat or kerosene had been stored. His elder sister's job was to fill water. He would accompany her to the river, the distance shrinking when they went, lengthening on their return. Empty vessels clanged musically as they skipped over dry earth, plucking karvandas from bushes, yanking themselves up trees for jamuns that turned mouths purple. On the return, hot rocks scorched their bare feet. Balancing heavy *handi*s slowed the pace. Rahul sometimes deliberately dropped a *handi* to cool the earth, but the momentary comfort gave way to rough terrain again. The first hut was as welcome a sight as the karvanda bushes on the way out.

Till the Odious One came into their life, bedtime was the eagerly awaited hour. His mother always managed an evening meal, however frugal. And however tough the day, she told her brood stories or sang to them. Rahul could hear her sad, plaintive voice in his head, even if her features were no longer easy to recall.

Dusting his pants he left the swing, making space for that blocked-out voice. Humming a melody whose words had long been forgotten, he let his feet drag him back to the huddled figure on the station bench, drifting into padlocked memory-land. A word wafted in, then a phrase, a line about star-crossed lovers. Rahul repeated them aloud as if meeting a long-lost friend. As he settled into an adjacent bench, the story came back in a flash. But not the lovers' names.

Once again he was lying beside his mother in their hut, one sister on her lap, the other at her breast. She was caressing their heads. It was his favourite legend about . . . oh, why couldn't he remember the names?

The heroine was the beloved of seven adoring brothers who pandered to her every whim. When it was time to get her married they couldn't bear to send her away, so they found a *ghar-jamai* instead. Then drought struck their village. Crops failed, cattle died. The distraught brothers went to the village *bhagat* who said the gods disapproved of a *ghar-jamai* and demanded human sacrifice. The brothers killed their brother-in-law in the fields, buried the body in a canal and told their sister her husband had run away. She was inconsolable and wandered around the village calling his name like a woman gone insane. One day she came across an embankment at the head of an irrigation canal. She was about to sit down when she spotted a finger sticking out of the mud. Screaming frantically she dug out her husband's decomposing body.

At this point of the story Rahul's mother invariably paused to wipe her eyes with a corner of her pallu. That movement was etched in Rahul's memory. Slowly, her hand would return to his head but her voice would crack as she resumed. Grief over her husband's death coupled with her brothers' treachery broke the woman's heart. Her world turned dark in the middle of day and she ended her life beside her beloved husband.

His mother would tell the story and sing the legend. Her voice tripped effortlessly over the notes. Rahul fell asleep on the station bench with her hand on his head, her voice in his ears, oblivious of the moon keeping watch.

Jitsu-Mitki. He awoke with the lovers' names on his lips, feeling rested. Day was breaking as the waning moon struggled to hold its contours against a greying sky. He was in no hurry to leave.

The woman on his bench was gone.

Tiny pink leaves gleamed in the early morning sunlight the day Kajol was to leave the hospital. It was the only peepul tree in the compound. Each February it sprouted translucent leaves that deepened into green within a week. As Aparna walked briskly up the steps she thought it a good omen that the peepul was resplendent with new birth on the day Kajol was being discharged.

But she was worried about Rahul. There was something unnatural about the way he doted on the baby. Not paternal, not quite brotherly. Something else . . . In seven years Aparna hadn't come across a boy as full of contrasts as Rahul. After being cured of scabies he had hung around her hungrily for weeks, dusting the chair before she sat, carrying her parcels, even gifting her bottles of Bisleri.

'Don't sell this,' she told him kindly. 'Tap water contains germs. People drinking it fall sick.' Taking the bottle, she pointed to a fleck floating in the water. 'See, it's not as clean as you think.'

He brought her another, making sure it had no floating flecks. This time she was firm. 'Haven't I told you tap water is not fit for drinking?' she admonished, emptying the bottle at his feet.

He was hurt, uncomprehending. Tap water was the

only clean water he knew. He ran away from Sharan. Victor told her he was sleeping in the station again, not always with the card players. Sometimes no one knew where he was, though he turned up to grab seats, collect bottles and papers. Weeks passed before he reappeared, this time shyly holding out a shell to Aparna. 'For you, didi. You like it?'

'It's beautiful, Rahul. Thanks,' she exclaimed, running a finger along its jagged edge. 'Have you been at the beach these days?' He grinned happily, basking in her approval.

'I'm going to put it on the windowsill where everybody can see it,' she said, giving it pride of place in the assortment of memorabilia that the boys brought in from time to time—a plastic flower, a stone resembling Ganesha, a terracotta figurine with broken arms.

Then Salim saw the shell. 'This is from Kerala. You don't find shells like this in Bombay. It must be from Shashi's stall.'

When Aparna questioned Rahul he was hurt again. She saw his crestfallen face but insisted he return the shell. He looked aghast and bolted, this time he stayed away for months. She had almost given up on him when he appeared in the most unexpected way: dragging her to the platform to rescue Kajol.

As the day of Kajol's discharge neared, Aparna tried to prepare him. To deepen his links with Sharan she got Shekhar to start training him as *bal-daktar*, even though he was still too young for the role. He enjoyed holding court with a plastic box of cotton wool, gauze and bandages as boys queued before him with their complaints. He had to distribute band-aids and Dettol after ascertaining that the cuts and bruises were genuine. When no one was looking he would slip Bablu an extra strip or two. They could sell them and share a Pepsi.

One day Bablu asked Rahul for two large bandages. 'Where are you hurt?' asked Rahul.

'Just give, yaar.'

Two hours later a grinning Bablu appeared with his left leg wreathed in blood-soaked bandages. 'What happened?' asked Rahul in alarm.

'I went to the mutton market. See how much I earn today.'

Rahul laughed. 'So give me a treat!'

That evening Bablu took Rahul far from Dadar. They took front seats on the upper level of a double-decker bus that squeezed into lanes teeming with shops, shops, and more shops whose wares veered dangerously close to the bus. Handcarts laden with fruit and shirts, plastic boxes and sari petticoats added to the space crunch. Bablu was in his element, leaning out of the window, leaving a trail of fingerprints on dusty hoardings. Before they got off, he yanked the roller indicating the bus's destination. At the next stop there was an uproar as commuters quarrelled about No. 124 going to Bhau Cha Dhakka instead of the Colaba bus station. Rahul had a hard time keeping a straight face as they jumped off.

It was an unknown area more crowded than Dadar, with dozens of pavement residents. Bablu led him to Amma, a dark, big-boned woman with pendulous breasts stirring a huge *dekchi* on red coals over a *sigri*. Sharp aromas wafted from her pot. Bablu handed her ten rupees and she spooned two helpings into tin plates battered shapeless by overuse. They were too hot to hold. Bablu placed his on the bonnet of a taxi and began tucking into the 'poor man's biryani'. Rahul's fingertips were scalded by the hot chicken and rice, pungent with raw spices. But he enjoyed the biryani.

Shuklaji Street had several women like Amma cooking for the street population. Lined by scrap dealers' shops whose boards announced weekly changing prices for paper, plastics, milk packets, Bisleri bottles, it was the ultimate destination for rag-pickers who recycled scrap from all over Bombay. Rahul noticed that the prices offered were higher than at Dadar and resolved to bring his next haul of paper and plastic here.

'Look,' winked Bablu, leading Rahul into a brightly lit lane overflowing with women. They leered, dark kohl in their eyes, grins on grimacing faces. Swinging arms attracted attention outside symmetrical doors below identical barred windows with more women peering out, dressed and half-dressed.

For a while they watched the circus of men coming and going into box-like doors that shut for a few minutes, then swung open again. The area throbbed with energy. Inexplicably, it left him cold. Much as he liked the biryani, he was in no hurry to return to Shuklaji Street.

He had become a regular at Heera-bai's stall, however, tucking into vada-pao with relish, developing a secret crush on the girl weaving *torans* and *venis*. The grey-haired woman, he learnt, was her grandmother. In the afternoon, when customers were few, she would make the girl sit beside her, rub oil into her hair and run a fine-toothed comb through it to weed out lice. Sometimes the girl rebelled, preferring to play with her brown-and-white cat. When Rahul heard the old woman calling 'Chandni! Eh, Chandni!' he discovered the girl's name.

He was dusting the desk at Sharan when the phone rang. 'Hel-lo,' began a tremulous voice. 'Is it 1098?'

'Yes, this is Childline,' replied Rahul. The phone went dead in his hand. He turned the receiver and looked into it, nonplussed.

'Who was it?' asked Victor from behind.

'I don't know. They put the phone down.'

'Maybe they didn't like your voice,' teased Bablu.

'What's wrong with my voice?'

'Like a girl's, yaar. They thought Childline would have someone big, important.'

'Not a *chutiya* like you,' snarled Salim, coming out of the bathroom. 'Puts on this act of being a father but has a girl's voice. Go get my clothes from the washing line!'

'I don't have a girl's voice,' said Rahul shrilly, ignoring the command.

'I-don't-have-a-girl's-voice,' mimicked Salim in a higher pitch.

Rahul lowered his head, ready to ram into Salim, when the phone rang again. Before Victor could reach it, Rahul lunged towards it and growled 'hello' in the deepest voice he could manage.

'Is this Childline? Can I speak to Aparna?' came a friendly female voice as Bablu and Salim chortled. Rahul was grinning too.

'Aparna-didi will come at eleven,' he said more confidently.

'Please tell her to phone the hospital.'

Rahul's eyes widened. 'Is . . . is anything wrong?'

'Are you the boy who comes with her?' Rahul nodded. The pause lengthened. 'Are you the same boy?'

'Y-yes,' stammered Rahul.

'What's your name?'

'Rahul.'

'Rahul, give Aparna a message, will you? Tell her baby has cut her first tooth.'

'What?'

'Tell Aparna the baby now has a tiny tooth in her lower jaw.'

'Tooth,' smiled Rahul, face relaxing, eyes glowing. 'Baby's got a tooth,' he whooped, dropping the phone and jumping on Bablu like a cricketer who's just taken a wicket. Bablu laughed, slapping palms with him in triumph.

Salim observed them disdainfully. '*Bakwas. Poora bakwas*,' he sneered, storming off.

Victor kept looking at Rahul thoughtfully. 'Stop getting so involved with the baby.'

'Why not! She's mine.'

'You'll feel awful when she's sent away.'

'She can't be sent away. Where will she go?'

'Didi will find a place for her.'

'She won't. She likes her as much as I do.'

Kajol was being transferred to Bal Kendra, an orphanage run by nuns who arranged for children to be adopted by families abroad, provided one parent was Indian. Aparna had visited the Kendra, satisfied herself that the babies were well looked after and had become friendly with the superintendent, Sister Margaret. She started preparing Rahul for Kajol's discharge.

'Kajol is well now. Other babies need her place,' she told him one morning as he carried her around in the hospital corridor.

'You're ready to come home,' said Rahul, burying his nose in Kajol's belly. The tickle made her giggle. 'I'll make a swing for you with didi's dupatta. I'll keep you next to me.'

The glimpse into his fantasy world jolted Aparna. 'We can't take Kajol to Sharan,' she said more sharply than she intended. 'Sharan is only for boys.'

He digested her words. 'So . . . where will she go?'

'To Bal Kendra. They look after babies.'

'Where is Bal Kendra?'

'At Vashi, New Bombay. It takes one hour by train.'

'So far . . .!' Rahul's voice was shrill.

'It's best for Kajol,' said Aparna gently. 'Let's hope she finds a family soon.'

Guiltily he remembered the woman on the bench. Should he tell Aparna about her? She would berate him for not mentioning it earlier.

'Will I . . . will I be able to see her?'

Aparna nodded. 'I've told Sister Margaret about you. You'll be allowed to see her once a week.'

'That's all?'

'Normally they don't allow visitors. They're making an exception.'

Rahul's mind had gone numb. The baby who had become the fulcrum of his life was being taken away. He would only see her once a week.

He left in a daze. Wandering aimlessly, he found himself in the park, deserted in the hot afternoon. The wooden plank of the swing scorched his thighs. He climbed on, standing, ignoring the metal chains burning his palms. Bending his knees, he started swinging higher and higher, eyes shut tight against the blazing sun, mind blank to all but the rhythm of the swing. He was barely aware of the tears running down his face. Higher and higher went the swing, carrying him above the pole that held its chains. Then the inevitable happened. The swing somersaulted over the pole. Losing his grip, Rahul landed with a thud in the mud; the swing crashed wildly into his head. He sat there hugging the swing, crying uncontrollably.

That night he gave up both Sharan and the bench. He returned to sleep on local trains that carried him to the last stop and back till he awoke. Like in the old days. Before Vicky. Before Bablu. Before Kajol. When he was alone.

For a boy based at Dadar station, Vashi was a world apart. Not only did Rahul have to change trains at Kurla, jostling between legs, buttocks and torsos, but Vashi was built on a different scale from all he was familiar with. Just after Govandi and Mankhurd, with their sprawling ramshackle sheds, the crowded local thundered over the long stretch of Thane Creek, and Rahul stared abstractedly at a spindly boatman steering a solitary boat in the water below. Distance shrank buses to toy-size on a parallel bridge. The train slowed as it approached mangrove marshlands and ground to a halt at Vashi.

He had been to VT, but the magnificent Gothic architecture did not overwhelm him because of the comforting crowds into which he dissolved. Vashi station, on the other hand, had no resident population. Tall walls loomed over Rahul, dwarfing him. He hugged Aparna's shadow, peering into glossy granite that reflected his silhouette.

There were no vendors in the street. Instead, fast-food stalls offered Chinese food, burgers, Pepsi. He followed Aparna past a cycle stand towards a queue where a hundred autos snaked between dividers before emerging onto the road, which was wider than half a dozen train tracks. At least ten Sharans would fit under a single flyover, thought Rahul, as the auto sped past yellow tourist buses lounging like caterpillars under a leaf. Shopping malls with glass façades, a few public buses and not even the hint of a traffic jam. Rahul shivered involuntarily. Navi Mumbai intimidated him. It had too few *sadak chhaap*s like him.

Bal Kendra was the second-last building at the end of a tree-lined lane, more friendly than the malls. Its wide driveway was lined by hibiscus bushes leading to a porch. The porch gave the building an old-fashioned air. Everything else was contemporary.

Rahul stood shyly beside Aparna as she paid the auto driver. She had given him her brother's old shirt and shorts for the special outing. She too was dressed better than usual. Not only was her hair in a ponytail instead of a plait, she wore sandals with heels rather than her usual kolhapuris.

They climbed seven stone steps, walked down a corridor and stopped in front of a polished brown door above which a board announced 'Superintendent'. Aparna gave her visiting card to the peon guarding the door. Rahul's impulse to run was growing by the minute. He stayed only because he didn't know the way back. And because he wanted to see Kajol.

Sister Margaret was short, plump and middle-aged; she wore a light grey nun's habit. Her twinkling eyes suggested mischief. 'So this is the bright young man who found our baby,' she began.

Rahul's chest swelled. No one had called him a bright young man before. 'I gave her her name also,' he blurted out. That was a new detail for Sister. Rahul proudly described the scene at the railway station, enlarging his own role as usual. 'If it were not for didi, baby would have died that day,' he ended, gazing at the silver cross dangling on a black string over Sister's chest. His inhibitions had evaporated.

'So now I have one hero and one heroine. Shall I direct a film?' joked Sister Margaret.

Rahul giggled, hiding his face in Aparna's dupatta. 'We've come to see Kajol,' he said, the dupatta covering the lower part of his face.

'What's that?' asked Sister Margaret, cocking a hand behind her ear. 'Did I hear you want to act with Kajol?'

Rahul collapsed in laughter. 'We want to see Kajol,' he gasped.

'I'm afraid no film stars live here. You'd better go home.'

'Baby. We want baby Kajol . . .'

'You want to put a baby into the film? Then she will become the heroine and you will be the extras.'

Rahul instantly liked Sister Margaret. Bal Kendra would be good for Kajol. But where was she? Would this funny lady ever take him to her?

They walked down a long corridor, Aparna's heels clicking. Rooms to their right were under the charge of middle-aged women in green-bordered saris. At Room No. 7, Sister Margaret stopped, beckoning to the attendant. 'How is the new baby?' she asked.

'Crying-crying,' replied the woman as she sized up the visitors.

'Can I see her?' asked Rahul eagerly.

The attendant hesitated. 'Not allowed.'

'We've made an exception for our hero,' said Sister Margaret. 'He can visit on Saturdays.'

He entered a room with pictures of cherubic children.

Each crib was painted with a nursery motif and had a dangling toy. Three were painted pink, the other three blue. A baby in a pink crib was crying. He walked up to the crib calling 'Hakku', his special greeting for Kajol. The crying stopped. As her eyes focussed, her features puckered and her legs wriggled. He picked her up. She snuggled into the crook between his neck and shoulder, shutting her eyes. With his free hand he hugged her.

'So cute, it's touching,' he heard Sister Margaret murmur as he took Kajol into the garden with the bright red hibiscus. She giggled as he tickled her cheek with a flower, then she grabbed it and crushed it in her tiny hand. Rahul plucked another and stuck it behind her ear. She groped; he laughed, shifting it closer. Her fingers closed over it, crushing again. It dropped into Rahul's palm. Soon the ground had a carpet of crushed hibiscus.

'Can I come tomorrow?' he beseeched Sister Margaret.

'Not tomorrow, hero. Saturday.'

'Saturday is six days away . . .' his voice trailed off.

Sister Margaret exchanged glances with Aparna. 'Okay, hero, just this week you can come on Wednesday,' she said kindly. 'Tomorrow Aparna is treating my hero to a film. Which one do you want to see?'

Rahul turned inquiringly to Aparna. This was an unexpected treat. But Kajol clung to Rahul, sobbing, kicking as they struggled to prise her away. By the time they left he was crying as well.

The next day he wanted to see a film starring Kajol but there was none showing at the nearby theatre. So Aparna took him for *Zubeida*, a film that opened with a mesmeric red dupatta floating in the sky. A dupatta that seductively changed form, folding into itself, billowing out in the breeze, dancing without a body to give it form. The sets were lavish, the costumes rich, Karishma Kapoor and Rekha bewitching. But the story was sad, about a boy's longing for his mother who died when he was three. Rahul cried during the film. As they left the theatre he held on to Aparna's hand.

That night he dreamt of a red dupatta, dreamt he was being cuddled in it as Kajol had been in Aparna's. Leaving bones behind on the bench, he melted into cotton wool clouds, warm against his skin, dupatta looping around his boneless body, splitting his head into a separate swirl that vapourized with bumps against sunbeams. A half moon sailed past a bright blue sky. The dupatta swallowed it up. Rahul held the cold moon against his belly. It stuck to his skin. He tore the dupatta to free himself of the moon. It was glued on fast. He banged the moon with clenched fists. Splinters slithered into his nose, toes, crept under his fingernails. His fingers clutched moon slivers.

Rahul fell off the bench, shivering.

seven

A parna had tried reuniting Rahul with his family, but it proved impossible. His mother was a migrant construction worker moving from site to site. The last location he remembered was a dam across a river. He didn't know which dam, which river. Just that it dried up in summer and flooded when it rained. Their hut was in an open field among huts of other workers. He was seven when he ran away.

Rahul could remember his father's funeral. The wails of women as the mutilated body was salvaged from the dam's base, blood-soaked cloth covering his face. A self-appointed pundit tonsured Rahul's head. Another worker led him to the pyre, burning torch in hand, and held down the child's hand till the wood caught flame. For three days neighbours provided food for his mother, his sisters and him. On the fourth his mother had to feed the community; it was mandatory for the peace of his father's soul. The labour contractor advanced the loan she begged for. And their poverty level dipped even lower.

The same contractor became the Odious One. Rahul had woken one night to grunting sounds and called for his mother. He was told to shut up by an unfamiliar male voice. He started crying. The same voice sounded harsher,

'*Chup baith nahin to tera sir phor dalunga.*' Rahul cried uncontrollably. Then a slap stung his face. He expected his mother to come rushing, to comfort him. She didn't, remaining supine in a corner of the hut, not on the mat beside his sister where she normally slept. He felt betrayed. He never forgave her.

He had no words to describe the experience to Aparna. Each time she asked why he had left home he fell silent. Or he ran away, to the park with the swings that would take him up and down, up and down, helping him forget.

After Kajol came into his life Aparna tried a different tack. 'See how helpless a child is alone. Don't you think Kajol should be with her family?' she asked, watching him jingle a rattle the baby lunged for.

'If her family cared they wouldn't have left her,' he replied tartly.

You think she can survive on her own? She nearly died, remember?'

He put down the rattle and smiled at Aparna. 'There are kind didis like you in this world.'

She laughed, touched. 'And good boys like you, Rahul.'

'So who needs families!'

She became serious again. 'All children need families, Rahul. And parents love children even if they can't be good about it because of circumstances.'

He made a face. 'Bablu says parents are all right, but only for a while. Children must escape.'

'Bablu visited his family four months ago. Don't you want to visit yours?'

'No.' The answer was clear and abrupt. He had walled off his past with impenetrable steel. Aparna wondered if he was misleading her by not giving the location of his village. Try as she did, she made no headway with him.

He hadn't run away after the first betrayal, just slunk outside the hut, crying. Only after the Odious One left did Rahul crawl in again. But he turned away from his mother.

He might have put up with the nightly grunts and squeals if she hadn't started feeding him as well. The larger portion of rice, the thicker chapatti, despite the smell of liquor that hung about him. One day she cooked a chicken brought by the Odious One. He ate it all, leaving only the gravy to be shared between the children and their mother. Watching Munni suck bones left in the Odious One's thali made Rahul's seven-year-old blood boil. His mother's silence infuriated him more.

The next day, for the first time, she confronted the Odious One. 'Bring two chickens today. One for you, one for the children,' she said.

He looked at her as if she had asked for the moon. And returned empty-handed.

She said nothing as he washed up, got into a lungi and sat down for his meal as usual. She remained sitting where she was. 'Get food,' he ordered.

'I haven't cooked,' she replied sullenly.

'Haven't cooked! Why?'

'You were to bring chicken.'

'I brought chicken yesterday. You think I'm a *lakhopati* that I can bring chicken-wicken every day!'

'I told you . . .'

'*You* told me? Who are you to tell me? Don't forget you are repaying a debt.'

Rahul saw tears drop off his mother's cheeks, staining her sari a deeper mud-red. She held her ground. 'You made me cook for you. My children slept hungry.'

'Is that my fault? You should have cooked for them.'

'I thought they'd get some chicken . . .'

'If you thought wrong it's not my fault. Now stop sulking and give my food.'

'I told you I haven't cooked.'

'Then start cooking!' he shouted, kicking away his thali. It clanged, rolling a short distance before clattering flat, upside down.

'No mother can see her children hungry,' she wept.

'Do you think I have pots of money to support your children? I have my own brood!'

'Then . . . why come here . . .?'

'Because you have a debt to repay! If I don't get food in fifteen minutes I'm going to change the figures in the account books.'

With that the Odious One grabbed his mother's hair and pushed her towards the cooking utensils. She stifled a scream as the kerosene can tipped over. Precious fuel spilt on the ground. Rahul felt enraged, watching her struggle to mop it up with Munni's old dress. He ran out to fetch dry leaves.

The Odious One was sitting on their neighbour's charpoy, chatting as if nothing was amiss. As Rahul ran back with a handful of leaves he called, 'Tell your mother to hurry. I'm hungry.'

So are we, Rahul wanted to reply, but he didn't have the guts. He peeled garlic for his mother, chopped chillies, ground them into a paste. He fanned the flickering leaves till the sticks caught flame and the fire started up. He watched his mother stir dal on the fire, then settle down to knead atta for chapattis.

The Odious One returned. He stood at the entrance of the hut, leering at Rahul's mother. 'Not ready yet?' he barked.

'You can see we're working.'

He was swaying unsteadily on his feet. He had evidently been drinking. 'Boy, get out,' he snapped at Rahul. 'If my food isn't ready I might as well have something else first.'

His mother gasped. 'Shut up. Not in front of the child.'

'That's why I'm telling him to get out,' he muttered, lunging towards her.

'Later,' she cried, backing off.

'This will teach you to keep my food ready,' he said, pinning her against the wall, his hand landing on her breast like a claw.

Watching his mother's anger morph into acquiescence was worse than all that had happened before. Rahul couldn't take any more. He picked up the heavy stone with which he had ground masalas and flung it at the Odious One with all his strength. He heard him gasp. He saw a trickle of blood streaming from the left temple. He saw him slump to the ground in a heap. He heard his mother scream, 'What have you done, *sala badmash*? What have you done?'

He whirled towards her, his eyes blazing accusingly. But he had no words. She was looking at the Odious Heap at her feet. That was his last image of her. He didn't want to know if the Heap was alive or dead. He didn't want to face his mother's betrayal. He had to run away.

eight

Karim-bhai had no objection to Rahul learning to ride on his bicycle, as long as he stayed away from traffic. That question didn't arise. Rahul couldn't even balance. Legs astride, he would wobble a few yards and then topple. Watching him, Karim-bhai laughed.

'Ride a bullock cart! Villagers are only fit for bullock carts,' he called as Rahul picked himself up for the umpteenth time.

'Why cart, I can ride the bull itself,' responded Rahul.

'The bull will throw you off and piss on you!'

'Shall I piss on your cycle?'

Eventually Karim-bhai helped, holding the cycle seat, running alongside, till Rahul learnt to balance. A week later the boy was flying down deserted streets each night, marvelling at the power of wheels.

Around the same time Aparna increased Rahul's duties as *bal-daktar*. He had to accompany Shekhar to the public hospital with its permanently overcrowded OPD to learn about procedures. Later he would have to take sick children on his own.

Rahul soon learnt that being street-dwellers as well as children was a double disadvantage even in a hospital. They were ignored. People who came after them were sent in before them. He was afraid that Manoj, who had been shivering through the nights for almost a week, might get a temperature again.

'What's the matter?' asked the doctor brusquely when they were finally in his cabin.

'He gets fever and shivering at night,' replied Shekhar.

'Does he have fever now?' asked the doctor without picking up a thermometer. Shekhar remained non-committal. 'Give him Crocin. Bring him back after a bath.'

'We've already given him Crocin.'

'Give him a bath. Next!'

'But doctor . . .'

'I have a roomful of patients. Stop wasting my time.'

Rahul was dismayed but Shekhar was obviously used to it. 'Because our children are treated so badly they avoid hospitals,' he told Rahul.

Rahul's role as assistant *bal-daktar* facilitated his friendship with Chandni. He had never spoken to her till the day she was bitten by a dog. He was at the vada-pao stall, positioned to peer into the flower market where Chandni's grandmother was sprinkling water over floral discs. Chandni was a little distance away, clutching her cat against her chest. The flower in her hair was a red jacunti. She didn't notice the three dogs fawning over a bitch in heat. Rahul watched in amusement as one snapped away a rival and mounted the bitch, tongue lolling red in delight. The rival bared his teeth with a nasty growl and the dog slipped out. The bitch ran off, three dogs following, tails wagging. She crawled into a large, round straw basket and sat expectantly, paws crossed, just a few feet away from Chandni.

The grandmother called, 'Get that *kutri* out of our basket!' Just then a stone hit one of the dogs. Rahul didn't see who had thrown it, but within seconds the dogs were snarling at one another. 'Eh, Chandni! Get rid of that *kutri!*' the old lady called again.

Chandni turned and, with the cat in one hand, tipped over the basket with the other. The bitch jumped out, three panting dogs at her heels. The first dog nosed her rump and mounted again. His rival's canines glinted under raised jowls, threatening a fight. The cat chose this moment to leap out of Chandni's arms towards the dogs. Chandni screamed and lunged for her cat. Rahul watched in horror as dogs, cat and Chandni's legs flailed amidst rising howls. Someone flung a bucket of water at the melee and the animals ran off. But Chandni's leg was bleeding. Vicious teeth had sunk into her flesh.

As Chandni lay in her grandmother's lap sobbing, Rahul grabbed the opportunity. 'I'm a *bal-daktar* at Sharan, ma-ji. I'll get medicine for that wound,' he said self-importantly, speeding off. Within minutes he was back with Dettol antiseptic cream. Blood ran down Chandni's leg, falling on the road in round, red drops.

'She'll need stitches,' murmured a flower seller.

'I know the hospital, ma-ji. I can take you,' volunteered Rahul.

They bandaged the leg in a stained cloth and helped Chandni limp to the hospital, tears streaming down her face. Rahul hurried them through a side entrance, cutting the distance to the OPD, only to find it closed. An attendant sat laconically on a bench, teeth red from chewing paan.

'My friend has been bitten by a dog. Her leg is bleeding,' said Rahul.

The attendant looked down at the leg. 'OPD timing is

51   *Sadak Chhaap*

ten o' clock in the morning to twelve. Come back then.'

Rahul clenched his teeth. 'It's only six-thirty. She'll bleed all night. She needs a doctor now,' he said in as firm a voice as he could manage.

The attendant looked amused. 'Doctor's gone home. You think he's going to come back for something so small?'

'Emergency is twenty-four hours.'

'This is not emergency. She won't die before morning.'

Rahul was livid. 'You can't talk to patients like that! Take us to a doctor immediately!' he cried, his self-confidence deflated. The attendant ignored him, returning to his papers on his table.

'Government hospitals are useless. I'll take her to a private doctor,' sighed Chandni's grandmother.

'Ma-ji, come to Sharan. My friend will know how to bandage her foot.' They made Chandni limp all the way back to Sharan, where Shekhar applied antiseptic cream and bandaged her foot. He advised her grandmother to take her for injections the next day.

Chandni smiled at Rahul as they were leaving. His heart soared.

Aparna was mistaken in hoping that keeping Rahul busy would divert his attention from Kajol. Saturday afternoons were reserved for the baby. He would wake up early, complete his chores and bathe before getting dressed. He never went empty-handed, taking her a flower, or a banana from Karim-bhai, or biscuits saved from teatime. Once in a while he would splurge on a Cadbury's bar. Rahul had a problem parting with Cadbury's. More than once it got gobbled up on the train journey to Bal Kendra.

Kajol now had six teeth in the lower jaw, four in the

upper. Her hair had changed from downy to thick. She was wobbling on her feet. After a few uncertain steps, she would land on the ground with a thud, looking surprised. Rahul would lift her to her feet and move a little distance away. When she ran into his arms he would swing her high into the air. She was a cheerful child, the only remnant of her trauma being a three-inch scar behind her left knee. From time to time Rahul would stroke the scar. It didn't evince even a twitch.

Late nights found him pedalling along Tulsipipe Road. In ten months he had shot up by six inches. His gangly legs sticking out of his shorts were still hairless but he could pedal without standing on his toes, swerve fast, brake suddenly and jump off a moving bike without smashing it into a wall. But the bicycles he used weren't always Karim-bhai's.

It was Salim, of all people, who taught him to pick a bicycle lock. He could use any cycle and replace it without suspicion. The owner was asleep anyway. The cycle would be back before it was needed. No harm, no loss and all was well, he reasoned in a child-adult way.

He was testing the brakes at top speed one night when his attention was arrested by raucous voices. Two women were bargaining heatedly. One rocked an infant rolled in a cloth slung between lamp post and railway fence. He could hear numbers being bandied back and forth. Then money changed hands and one woman handed over the baby to the other.

'You can't sell your baby!' yelled Rahul, slamming the bike to a halt within inches of the women.

'Mind your own business,' snapped one of the women.

'The baby could be my sister. Don't sell her!'

'I haven't sold her, *chutiya*. I've hired her out for a day. She has to start earning.'

'Babies can't work,' he said defensively.

'They can beg, no, *ullu*?' mocked the woman.

Rahul leaned on the bike, nonplussed. 'Why don't you beg with your own baby?'

'Some nights I earn differently. What's your problem if my sister earns instead?' Seeing his stupefied face, both women laughed. 'Come to me when you're ready,' called the first woman, lowering her pallu and jiggling her breasts. Rahul felt a tightness in his crotch. Awkwardly, he cycled away. As he settled into his bench at night the image of the jiggling breasts kept popping up. Even the red-orange setting moon couldn't drive it away.

The same moon was mocking him as it sailed through silver clouds the night Murugan was brought to Sharan by a railway official who had found him loitering at the station, looking lost. He had recently arrived from Andhra Pradesh, spoke neither Hindi nor Marathi and had a large, black sore on his foot. When a green tinge appeared at the edge, Aparna asked Rahul to take him to hospital. Rahul advised Murugan to bathe and borrow clean clothes.

'What's this undu-gundu, undu-gundu? Can't you speak a proper language?' barked the doctor whose name, Rahul learnt, was Paralkar. Rahul helped Murugan raise the painful leg to the examination table. Dr Paralkar put on latex gloves. Selecting a steel instrument from a tray he bent over the leg—and withdrew as if stung. 'The wound is full of maggots. Get him off my table!' he ordered brusquely.

'He's in pain, doctor . . .'

'Get him out at once! Before he infects the place! Remove the maggots and bring him back fast or we'll have to cut off his leg.'

Rahul was angry but frightened. How dare the doctor be so rude! What were maggots? How was he supposed to remove them? What would it be like for Murugan to become *apang* overnight? Be a *langda* all his life? He helped Murugan hobble back. His voice was shrill with indignation as he narrated their experience, but again Shekhar was stoic. 'In two cases we ourselves had to remove maggots with tweezers. I'll get three-four boys to help.'

It was like a mini-surgery conducted without anaesthesia. Four boys held a writhing Murugan while Shekhar removed maggots one by one with tweezers heated over a candle flame and wiped clean with Dettol. Rahul watched with horror and fascination as maggot after wriggling maggot dropped into a tin of Dettol-spiked water. Blood-curdling shrieks emanated from Murugan, curses in a language they did not understand. The frenzy of the worms in Dettol matched the frenzy of the screaming boy. After it was over Rahul vomited.

There was no moon to curse that night. The thin sliver had risen and set before Rahul reached his bench. He sat with knees hunched, staring into the blackness between rail tracks. He dreaded taking Murugan to hospital the next day, shivering as the face of the doctor swam into memory. Rahul imagined the horrendous man brandishing a long knife and hacking at Murugan's leg. He imagined poor Murugan screaming and writhing while Rahul stood by, mute and helpless, in a room full of blood.

He had had enough of playing *bal-daktar*, he decided. At next Friday's meeting he would resign. But Friday was four days away. If they waited that long Murugan would lose his leg. Should he feign illness or abscond? Rahul weighed the options, staring into the black emptiness between parallel tracks that stretched endlessly, connecting city to wilderness, wilderness to village. Hard unyielding tracks set on hard unyielding sleepers. Tracks that trapped from point to point, allowing no change of direction. Like lines on palms. Destiny Lines.

He slept fitfully, waking with each passing train. The rhythmic rattling soothed with its predictability, reminding him that passengers reaching their destinations safely outnumbered those maimed in mishaps, its capacity to maim overshadowed by its capacity to transport. Night overpowered by dawn.

At the first sign of light Rahul was up. Mechanically he folded his sheet and headed for the public toilet. Then he turned back. He would use Sharan's toilet for the last time. He had to pick up his sack.

At Sharan the boys were up, morosely making tea. 'Murugan is going to die,' Bablu told Rahul. 'Whole night he was shouting-shouting. Shekhar took him to hospital at two o'clock.'

Though a little guilty, Rahul felt relieved. He wouldn't have to face the doctor. He wouldn't have to leave Sharan. He joined the others in their vigil. He hoped Murugan wouldn't lose his leg.

On a day when Vashi's cycle stand was deserted, Rahul put his secret plan into practice without any actual planning. For weeks he had observed cycles standing patiently, waiting for owners day after day. They looked bored, longing for adventure, but stuck in their niche along the wall. That day they did not even have a chana-wallah for company. As Rahul walked up to the stand, the sun gleaming off a handlebar made the cycle smile. Looking around he took out a piece of wire, bent over and opened a lock. Casually he wheeled out the bicycle and mounted. Soon he was flying down streets with autos and cars. Competition for speed was heady. He cycled along the left, obeying red and green lights, testing speed whenever the road was clear. He parked a block before Bal Kendra.

Cycling to the Kendra saved bus fare, enough to treat himself to an ice-gola from a handcart. His eyes would roll watching the vendor shave a block of ice over a speckled serrated blade, mould crushed ice into a ball over a stick and douse it with sweet red or tangy green sherbet. The golas left Rahul with colourful moustaches that kept his tongue busy, as cool waves rolled all the way down to his stomach.

Soon cycling became routine and Rahul abandoned all caution, walking up to the cycle stand like a seasoned commuter, approaching cycles with the careless ease of an owner.

Then the inevitable happened. On a day when Rahul's face was a sticky red, his clothes shabby, with an unmistakable *sadak chhaap* odour, his walk appeared too cocky to the commuter behind him. Rahul was seen picking the lock, and the cry went up, '*Chor! Chor!*'

A crowd gathered. There was no escape. He tried to explain that he was only borrowing the bike, that it would be returned before it was needed. His plea found no takers. He was handed over to a security guard, who stopped a police van that sped away carrying Rahul to a sector of Vashi he had never seen.

He refused to give his name, age or local address. 'We'll find out about your gang even if we have to thrash you,' snarled the moustached police officer, weighing the possibility of a confession leading to bigger arrests. He took Rahul to an interrogation room where two cops towered over a man with bloodshot eyes, wrists in handcuffs. As a lathi came down, the man yelped. 'You'll get the same treatment unless you talk,' said the cop.

There was no gang to tell about. The cop didn't believe him. One whack had Rahul howling. With the second he begged for Sister Margaret. The cop looked at him in disbelief. As a mere formality he phoned Bal Kendra.

'A bicycle thief claims you know him,' he began laconically.

'We look after babies, not thieves,' came an icy voice.

'Do you have a baby called Kajol?'

'Oh, my goodness! That's our hero!'

One thousand bodies fused into a giant amoeba writhing on the open-air dance floor. Tall gangly teenagers competed for space with six- and eight-year-olds, while older boys vied to dance opposite a handful of girls.

'I'm the best, I'm the best, I'm—the—best . . .' went the lyrics, at top volume.

Feet stomped to an insistent rhythm, made more demanding by strobe lights bouncing off eyes, teeth and the brightest of clothing. A rhythm that penetrated and energized bodies, releasing minds from tarnished dreams.

As always, Rahul danced like one possessed, imitating Shah Rukh, Govinda and other film stars. Beside him danced an older boy in jeans and dark glasses. For a minute their movements synchronized, then the boy swayed away, waving to a hand above bouncing heads. Rahul danced on. Music affected him viscerally. He heard it in his guts, not his ears. The moment the boom-boom-boom started, his knees rocked, his spine swayed and his legs carried him to the dance floor, hips swaying, pelvis thrusting, hands flying through air with an energy of their own.

He never missed the mela for street kids at the Don Bosco shelter on the twentieth of each month. The full-day jam session with video films for free was the high point of his month. Only the Childline annual party was bigger. It brought together kids from all parts of the city. With a feast of biryani, ice cream, cola and other goodies.

Today Rahul's heart wasn't into dancing. It wasn't with Kajol either. His heart had its reason for staying aloof, a reason that pivoted around Rahul alone. It was his last week at Sharan. The nearest to any home he had known. A place where he knew he wouldn't be rejected. Though he rarely slept there, it held his network of friends.

Bicycle images danced in his head. He could have kicked and smashed them all. Clenching his fists, he jabbed the air—in front, to the sides, up and down. One incident was changing his life, taking him away from almost everyone he knew. Tentative trust built over months dissolved with changes in attitude.

The most palpable change was in Aparna. Sister Margaret's call had shaken her up. 'How could you do such a thing, Rahul?' she cried in anguish as he stood before her. His explanation of 'borrowing not stealing' cut no ice with her. 'Today it's a cycle, tomorrow it could be something bigger. You could be locked up in a remand home for months. Is that what you want?'

Rahul shuddered. That was the worst threat she could have made. The overcrowded, understaffed remand home was a house of horror according to any child who had been there. Salim had escaped by bribing a guard. And Aparna hadn't sent him back.

'I want to keep you out of the remand home,' she continued. 'But for that I need your cooperation. From now on show me your train and bus tickets when you go to Vashi. And tell me who you meet, what you do. Be careful you don't get into bad company.'

Rahul didn't answer. Without the freedom to come and go as he pleased, Sharan lost its attraction. He began avoiding Aparna, shutting off from the hurt in her eyes.

She was dancing at the far end of the dance floor, ponytail flapping as the music pounded *Koi mil gaya*. She caught his eye and waved. He waved back but turned away, to find himself facing Bablu, hands slithering imaginary ripples, feet double-pacing the music as he combined bhangra with disco. He would miss Bablu. He alone had argued on his behalf. 'It's not *chori*, it's *masti*,' he told Aparna, who thought she knew better. 'Even Lord Krishna used to steal buttermilk from *gopi*s.'

Rahul felt pleased with that. But Karim-bhai was unimpressed. 'Krishna can get away with anything because he's a god. If I'd known cycling was going to get you into trouble I'd never have let you learn.' Karim-bhai wouldn't give him the cycle again.

Victor had been more amused than shocked. 'Borrowing, stealing, it's all part of life,' he said, putting a brotherly arm around Rahul.

Only Salim was impressed. 'Despite your *naqli*-papa nonsense you might get somewhere after all, *chutiya*,' he told Rahul with a glint in his eye.

Salim was nowhere to be seen at the party. But Rahul spotted Chandni in a green-and-yellow *ghaghra-choli* embroidered with gaudy gold, a shiny gold clip holding champa flowers instead of jacunti in her hair. The sight of her sparked electric currents through him and he gyrated into contortions and convolutions that had boys circling him, clapping to the histrionics of his boneless body. For that moment he imagined he was on stage with Govinda—cheered and catapulted to stardom.

The fantasy propelled him to the edge of the dance floor where Chandni was sitting with two girls and a loaded paper plate. 'Can I have wafers?' he called, stretching out his hand. She extended the plate. The dance floor erupted with wolf whistles. Her friends tittered. Rahul danced away, dreaming of being spotted by a film producer, dancing in song-dance sequences of films with Chandni beside him.

The moment passed. Depression returned. Though his

body kept moving, his mind turned inward again.

Sister Margaret's way of correcting had been different from Aparna's. She had reached the police station within half an hour and was locked in the officer's cabin as Rahul waited in trepidation outside. Emerging grim-faced, she led him to Bal Kendra's Sumo and hustled him in. At the Kendra he was ushered into the parlour, a small square room with four chairs around a square table. Stark and bare. A picture on a wall showed a serene-faced mother holding a small child. Both heads had golden auras around them.

The wait seemed interminable. When finally Sister Margaret appeared, the ever-present twinkle in her eye was gone. 'I went to the chapel to pray for you,' she said, taking the chair opposite him. For the next hour she probed and prodded till she had extracted a full confession. Relenting slightly, she called him to her side of the table and made him go down on his knees. A strange posture, one he had never tried before. It made him feel wobbly. She held out the silver cross hanging from her neck towards him. It had a man with a suffering face, his arms stretched along the horizontal axis.

'Hold the cross in your right hand, close your eyes and repeat what I say,' instructed Sister Margaret. Rahul obeyed.

'Forgive me for having sinned in your eyes, dear Jesus. Help me become a good boy again. Mother Mary, pray for me. Help me become a good boy again.'

He opened his eyes as she took back the cross. Relieved to see the hint of a smile. But who were Jesus and Mary? What was 'sin'?

There was no question of returning to Sharan unescorted. Sister Margaret had informed Aparna. Someone was on his way to fetch him. Rahul asked if he could see Kajol. Sister Margaret shook her head. 'No visits for a week. And if you misbehave again, your visits will be terminated.' There was nothing to do but sit morosely on the steps till Shekhar arrived.

Shekhar had tried to stymie the move to shift Rahul to Bal Kendra. Rahul had become an invaluable helper. But Shekhar was a street kid turned social worker without formal education. Sister Margaret and Aparna knew better.

'*Papa kehte hai bada naam karega . . .*' Rahul let the song reconnect body and mind, throwing himself into the pulsating rhythm. Although his image of 'papa' was flimsy, for the past week he had been told he was moving up in the world. That he was being given a job paying nine hundred rupees per month with food and shelter provided. That half the station population would kill for such a job. That he was the luckiest boy in the world. He had every reason to celebrate.

Then why was he feeling low?

All the blossoms on the hibiscus tree had shrivelled into ugly shapes and were drooping. The previous evening they had been blooming, bright and red. Rahul couldn't understand it. One or two droopy flowers was natural, but the entire bush? Despondently he began plucking the sad flowers, thinking that his first day at Bal Kendra was starting badly.

'What are you doing?' called Anthony, the elderly mali, his glazed eyes suggesting blurred vision.

'Removing dead flowers.'

'They're not dead, *gadha*! What do you know about gardens? Wait two hours and see what is dead, what is alive.'

Sure enough, two hours later the flowers had regained form and bounce, long tongues hanging out to tempt bees.

'Some flowers sleep at night, like people,' explained Anthony. 'Sunlight wakes them up. For watering, early morning is best. Never water when sun is high. Groundwater gets hot and burns tender roots.'

He was to be Anthony's assistant, tending the garden and the vegetable patch outside the kitchen where the Kendra grew tomatoes, chillies, beans. Two spindly trees shaded the vegetable patch, one with small white flowers and long drumsticks, the other with green and yellow guavas. Rahul's impulse was to climb the guava tree and bite into the ripening fruit. It had been ages since he had climbed a tree.

Weeding was a boring, repetitive chore. Despite having had their heads chopped off, defiant roots clung to the earth and threatened to sprout fresh green. But watering was fun. Jabbing his thumb into the mouth of the hose Rahul could flash jets at distant plants, make water leap to high windows, marvel as morning rays converted droplets into diamond showers.

'Did you really live at a railway station before coming here?' An older boy was looking at Rahul with wonder as he swept dry leaves in the garden. When Rahul nodded he sprang another question. 'Were you a goonda?'

'No,' laughed Rahul. 'I just slept there. And worked.'

'Worked?'

The boy's eyes grew wide as Rahul told him about grabbing seats, selling water, becoming *arogya mantri* at Sharan. Venkatesh laughed. 'Child *mantris* . . . what next?' he said, shaking his head.

Venkat was the oldest boy at Bal Kendra. He was also the darkest. His was not the tanned skin of children growing up under the sun but a deeper, denser pigment. The whites of his eyes shone brightly in contrast as he lapped up nuggets about Rahul's early life, coloured with imaginative drama. Venkat had no memory of his parents. He had grown up in a series of orphanages; his spell at Bal Kendra was the longest. At nineteen, in his final year of school, he was flirting with the idea of moving out.

Bal Kendra housed forty-odd children, most of them under five. Babies were kept in nurseries, older kids in dormitories. For the first week Rahul shared Anthony's small shed behind the kitchen garden. Then he was shifted into a dormitory with seven other boys. He ate with the older children in a pantry next to the kitchen. The food was tasty, with fish on Fridays and chicken on Sundays. Rahul enjoyed the flaky flavour of fish and the spicy coconut curries in which it was cooked. But most of all he enjoyed the feeling of importance as he sat on a bench and ate off a table. At Sharan everyone ate on the floor.

'If you're not having papad, pass it to me.'

Rahul turned to the boy beside him. 'I'm eating it last,' he said.

'Why? Papad is to be eaten with food. It's not pudding.'

'Pud-ding. . .' He liked the sound of the word. Like the tinkle of a bell. Did pud-dings crackle like papad, he wondered. 'I can have papad-pud-ding,' he declared.

The boy grinned. 'I make papad-kachumbar. Sprinkle it over rice. Want to try?'

Rahul was disappointed at the concoction. It added crunch to the rice but soon became soggy. He preferred papad crisp.

He had not noticed a crutch leaning against the wall. As they pushed back the bench, Gopi slipped it under his armpit and hobbled off. Rahul saw that his left leg was deformed: thin as a stick above the ankle, then a round ball replacing what should have been sole and toes. His throat constricted watching Gopi's jerky movements as he left the dining room.

The best part of being at Bal Kendra was seeing Kajol every day. She had started following him around just as Munni used to. Every evening he would choose her dress for the next day. And come to the nursery to find her bathed, dressed and spruced up for her outing in the garden.

'What's so special about this child? She's like any other.'

Rahul whirled. 'She's mine. I found her.'

Gopi suppressed a scornful laugh. 'Not for long. She'll go. Like the others.'

'She won't.'

Gopi looked at him pityingly. 'There's only one way you can keep her.'

'Which is?'

'Twist her leg.'

'Are you mad!' cried Rahul, his arm tightening around Kajol.

Gopi shrugged wryly. 'Nobody adopts a crippled child.'

Rahul was tongue-tied at the harsh words. 'Is that why you're still here?' he croaked.

A shadow darkened Gopi's face. He kept staring at Kajol with an expression Rahul could not fathom. 'My mother kept me when I was small,' he said at last. 'When I became too big to carry she would leave me in the hut. I would cry because children called me *kobij*, cabbage-foot. Then a Christian priest told my mother to put me in boarding. Every Diwali she brings jalebis for me.'

It was Sister Margaret who changed his nickname to Gopi, enchanted by Krishna, the god who led Arjun into the battle of Kurukshetra. 'You will face life's battles with courage, Gopi,' she would tell him as she filled up forms for his school. With a few others who didn't get adopted, he went to the Sacred Heart School and had reached sixth standard without repeating a single class.

The evening, between five and six, was Rahul's time for Kajol but he stole up to the nursery whenever he was free. If she was asleep he would settle down beside the tub of toys and pull out one after the other—teddy bears that felt soft against his cheek, ducks that quacked and flapped wings, horses that could be pulled on a string. Sometimes he thought of Munni, who had no toys. Except the parrot in a cage belonging to their neighbour. The parrot's cage hung from a tree. It would squawk as it was brought down. If they gave it karvandas it made approving sounds. But Munni wanted to pet the parrot. She poked her fingers between the bars, getting pecked again and again. To teach the parrot a lesson for making Munni's fingers bleed, Rahul had shoved a chilli into the cage. A hot green chilli with white seeds.

He liked making a house, cars, trains with colourful blocks. Their varied shapes and sizes could be used in so many ways. 'You're an intelligent boy, hero,' complimented Sister Margaret. 'Are you going to become a mechanic or an engineer?'

'Engineer,' replied Rahul, thinking it would be fun to drive fast engines.

'So tomorrow make me a bridge, okay?'

That didn't make sense. What did a bridge have to do with driving engines? But he made a bridge with a train racing over it. She was impressed. She summoned Rahul to the parlour and voiced her plans for his future. 'You know I've brought you here because the station environment isn't good for you,' she began.

He knew he was supposed to agree, so he nodded.

'We want to help you grow into a healthy young man who can hold his head high. You could work in an office, become a teacher, businessman, engineer. But the first thing is to get you into school.'

His eyes widened. He had never attended school. Wasn't it too late?

She had thought it all out. 'Since you can't read or write you can't get in with boys your age and if you are with small children you'll be miserable. I've asked Sister Angelina to coach you for two hours every morning. She will give you books, pencils, everything. If you study well, in one or two years you'll be ready for school. Wouldn't you like that?'

He nodded dutifully, sensing she was trying to help him.

Each morning as Rahul watered plants he would raise the jet to the guava tree, trying to make the guavas fall. But the best ones hung on, growing larger and yellower. Some were within reach of a tall person, but the ripe ones were higher. As temptation grew, Rahul knew he would have to climb. He decided to take his chance on an afternoon when children were at school and attendants asleep. Hearing Anthony snoring in the shed, Rahul strolled past the vegetable patch, leaning against the white trunk of the guava, planning foot and hand holds. Glancing around casually he hoisted himself up to the topmost branch, which swayed precariously with his weight. Balancing between branches, he munched two guavas, soft and sweet. He felt king of the world as he looked down at the vegetable patch, then gazed wistfully at a bus careening at top speed beyond the walls of Bal Kendra.

Then he spied the big one, just out of reach from his perch. He tested the stretch of his hand. Holding the branch, he inched closer. The yellow guava was still a foot away. Rahul crawled into a horizontal position and stretched again. His fingers closed over the fruit and the branch snapped. A portion of the tree crashed down in a whoosh.

Rahul was more startled than hurt, fingers still gripping the guava. Anthony ran out in a flash. No time to escape. Or think up an excuse.

'Don't you get enough food?' Sister Margaret's voice was reproving as she examined the broken branch laden with guavas. He looked down at his bruised feet. 'Next time you want something, ask, don't steal,' she said, and walked away.

He had to pluck all the guavas off the fallen branch and give them to Jessie the cook. She made him wash and cut them, then immerse them in a solution of jaggery. Stirring the brew over the stove made a sweet preparation. Kajol licked her lips but Rahul found the jam too sweet and staid—he missed the salt and chilli powder with which guavas were sold at the station.

He also missed his friends at Sharan terribly, especially Vicky and his comrade-in-pranks, Bablu. Bablu could contort his body into hideous postures and shiver like a palsied man. Or tie up a leg under dangling pants and hobble on a makeshift crutch. Or strike up a wail, 'My mother has just died . . . Come see her body . . . Please give money for her cremation . . .' His acting earned less than his creativity deserved. Life at the Kendra was comfortable but boring, and boredom was a state Rahul had never known.

eleven

A s his first month at Bal Kendra neared its end, Rahul looked forward to his first salary. He had learnt to sign his name. He could write numbers till fifty and was beginning to read simple words. He couldn't wait to show off his skills to Bablu, whom he had met only once since he had moved away. That had been a disaster.

Leaving the Kendra during the day was out of the question. His outings were monitored, the watchman told to report any wayward move. So one night Rahul shinnied up a tree and jumped over the wall after everyone, including the watchman, was asleep. What a sense of abandon he felt being in the street, unfettered, unescorted. He skipped to the bus stop and caught a train, ticketless, whistling *Hum tum ek kamre mein bandh ho* as Navi Mumbai's lights receded. Even the moon was in a mischievous mood, dancing to the rhythm of the train. At Dadar he lingered nostalgically around his bench. He was getting used to a mattress. The bench was part of his past.

He ran the entire length of the platform, thankful he hadn't lost speed. Only a few women remained at the flower market, packing droopy flowers into straw baskets, sweeping away crushed petals and leaves. Most stalls were shut at this hour, but at Sharan no one was asleep.

'*Aya! Apna hero aa gaya*!' whooped the boys as they surrounded Rahul. It was a homecoming like the parable of the prodigal son, where the fatted calf was cooked in celebration of the son's return.

He had learnt about the prodigal son from Sister Margaret who periodically told him stories with a moral ending, many of which made heroes of poor people like him. He particularly liked the parable of the Good Samaritan, in which several high-class people called Pharisees passed by a dying man on the road indifferently, but an ordinary man stopped and took him to a hotel called an inn, fed him and saved his life. When Sister Margaret asked who was the better person, Rahul had no hesitation answering it was the gentile, which is how she referred to the ordinary man. The indifference of the rich had a ring of truth to it. And the heroic compassion of the gentile made him feel good about being poor.

She also told him stories about Jesus, whom she worshipped along with his mother, Mary. While Rahul was touched by the veneration of motherhood, Sister Margaret's stories made Jesus sound more like a magician than a god. He could walk on water, make blind people see by touching their eyes and he managed to feed an extraordinary number of people from just five loaves of bread. Rahul would have liked to meet this Jesus.

Bal Kendra was forgotten now, as he caught up with his Sharan friends. They could only give him tea but the strong brew was a welcome change from the milky, tepid beverage he was getting at the Kendra. The notice board had photographs of the Don Bosco party. He spotted himself with an unknown boy raising a thumbs-up sign over his head. Rahul had no recollection of the boy but he was pleased to still be part of Sharan.

That night as he shared Bablu's bedroll, for the first time the odour that assaulted his nostrils felt unpleasant. 'Why don't you wash your clothes?' he said, turning his face towards the wall.

'What's come over you?' asked Bablu, aghast. 'Next you'll be saying have a bath.'

'I have one every day.'

'Oh-ho, so you've become a five-star-wallah . . .'

'*Chhod* yaar. What's wrong with having a bath?'

'What's-wrong-with-having-a-bath,' mimicked Bablu. 'Already forgotten how difficult it is to get water in the streets?'

'I've started a new life.'

'New-life . . .' mocked Bablu. 'Then why did you come back? To show off your new clothes?'

'Stop it!'

'What else? Coming in the middle of the night with your clean-clean face and clean-clean clothes. Do you even use perfume like Kapil in the Palmolive ad?'

'Shut up!'

'Meet *sadak chhaap* Rahul who now wears fancy shoes like Sachin, shirts like . . .'

'You're jealous, that's what!'

'Jealous? Of a *chutiya* like you?'

Coming from Bablu, that was a slap. Fighting tears, Rahul ran out of Sharan. Bablu calling him *chutiya* was unimaginable. They had never had a serious fight before. Was he wrong in trying to improve himself? Would it damage their friendship? What was wrong with having a bath? Weren't Victor and Shekhar constantly talking about being clean?

Something told him jealousy was the issue, not cleanliness. To keep Bablu's friendship he would have to share his luck. He glanced at the moon sailing through clouds at the same speed as the train. As the carriages crawled past the dark, silent waters of Thane Creek, Rahul made a decision: he would buy Bablu a gift. Bablu would be surprised and happy. Bablu was his best friend, too precious to lose. He jumped off the train feeling lighter.

He managed to slip past the dozing watchman, but in the dormitory Venkat was awake. 'Where have you been?' he hissed, keeping his voice low.

'Don't tell anyone . . . please. . .'

Only the white of Venkat's eyeballs gleamed in the pale light of the waning moon. Rahul sensed excitement in them. 'I will, unless . . .'

'Unless what?'

'Unless you take me next time.'

Rahul curled into bed, relieved.

He had decided to buy Bablu a brand new shirt, treat him to a film and ice cream. They could see *Border* for the twelfth time, or *Hum Apke Hai Kaun* for the seventh, or even the teary *Devdas*, which he had seen only twice.

First he had to collect his salary. Sister Margaret was waiting for him in the parlour. 'So, hero, how do you plan to use your hard-earned money?' she asked, her eyes twinkling.

He grinned, eyeing the white envelope on the table. 'I'm going to buy Bablu a shirt and take him to a movie,' he said.

'Wonderful. How much will that cost?'

'I dunno . . . We'll have ice cream and Pepsi.'

'Be sensible, Rahul. It's taken a whole month to earn this. Don't blow it up.'

He had always spent his money in a day or two, he wanted to tell her. Even when he found a wallet loaded with much more than nine hundred rupees. It would get stolen if he didn't spend it. In the streets there was no safe place to keep money, especially while you slept.

'You should start a post office account,' Sister Margaret was saying. 'Your money will earn interest. After a year you'll have some capital.'

Her words were going over his head. Besides, he was in no mood for advice. It was his money. He had worked for it. He needed it to make up with Bablu. She had to give it to him. She did, after some wrangling. Rahul saw disappointment on her face but he didn't care. No one was going to tell him what to do with his money.

He wavered between Hamid's stall and that of his rival across the road. Hamid sold shirts, his rival T-shirts. Bablu would love a Ganguly T-shirt. He could buy a blue Ganguly for Bablu and a red Sachin for himself. Two great cricketers, two great captains, one team. He felt chuffed buying the T-shirts, watching Hamid glare as he deliberately counted his notes in full view. '*Sala* show-off,' Rahul heard Hamid mutter as he slung the plastic bag over his shoulder, proud that he had stirred envy.

Predictably, Bablu was mollified. 'You are my best friend, yaar,' he said, holding the shirt against himself. It was too loose, too long, but the boys didn't care. 'You want me to have a bath before I wear it?' Rahul shrugged.

They saw *Chori Chori Chupke Chupke* and gorged on popcorn and ice cream, their earlier spat forgotten. As they stepped out of the theatre Bablu linked an arm through Rahul's. 'You'll take me to films again, no?' he asked. Rahul smiled.

After meeting Gopi, Bablu's pranks at playing lame made Rahul uncomfortable. He told Bablu about Gopi, how he kept pace with children going to school despite his crutch, only his awkward gait setting him apart.

'Is he in pain?' asked Bablu.

'I don't think so,' replied Rahul thoughtfully.

'Then he's better off than me. He lives in a proper house, goes to school.'

'But we shouldn't make fun—'

'Who's making fun! Just because you've started living in a palace you've become soft. The rest of us still have to survive.'

After the film Bablu wanted to walk on Mahim beach. But Rahul refused. 'I have to be back by eight,' he said ruefully.

'Why?'

'Dinnertime.'

'So? You've got money. We can eat on the beach.'

'I'll get into trouble.'

'With who? Your dadi?' Rahul kept quiet. 'Go. Listen to her. Become a big shot like she wants.' Drawing phlegm from the back of his throat Bablu spat on the road. Rahul returned to Bal Kendra in a happy but pensive mood.

Rahul and Gopi had worked out a deal. While vegetables, dal, rice, and chapattis were served in unlimited quantities, chicken, fish and dessert were limited to one portion per head. Gopi hated the smell of fish curry; roast chicken cooked without spices was too bland for Rahul. So they traded chicken for fish. Pud-ding, Rahul learnt, referred to a variety of sweet dishes served on weekends and holidays. Kheer was one of them, pink custard another. And when it was hot they got ice cream. Everyone wanted more pudding.

The first time Rahul swiped Gopi's ice cream it went unnoticed. Gopi went to wash his hands and returned to find his bowl empty. A few days later Gopi's kheer disappeared. Then the sev-korma. Gopi reported to Jessie, who kept watch. And Rahul was caught red-handed.

'How can you steal from a handicapped child!' scolded Sister Margaret, her eyes flashing. 'A hero must be noble, brave, not stoop to meanness!'

As she turned her back he heard her telling Jessie, 'Urchins are never satisfied. Give them an inch and they want a yard.'

After much cajoling he agreed to a night out with Venkat. Like the previous time, he crept down the stairs after everyone was asleep and led the way to the drumstick tree whose branches dipped over the wall. A hoist and a jump, and the boys were out, Venkat barely able to contain his excitement.

'Where do you want to go?' asked Rahul as they neared the station.

'To girls,' came the prompt reply.

Rahul considered this, remembering girls standing outside matchbox doors with dark red lips and kajal in their eyes near Shuklaji Street. They got off at Grant Road station and made their way to the city's most sexually active street. Girls hung around in twos and threes dressed in the gaudiest of colours, swinging arms provocatively. The younger ones wore *ghaghra*s with 'fevicol *choli*s' revealing every curve. Older women draped saris over bare midriffs. They leered as much as the men.

Two men stopped in front of a woman in a pink *ghaghra*. The boys heard them haggling. Then the woman called to a girl as young as themselves. She led both men into a room behind a flimsy curtain.

'They're going to do *ishq*,' whispered Venkat excitedly. Rahul nodded, feeling a stirring in his groin. 'Let's try.'

Rahul hesitated. The image of the woman jiggling her breasts often came to mind. But something held him back. 'Next time,' he mumbled. 'We'll miss the last train.'

Reluctantly Venkat turned, but a palpable excitement seethed through him all the way back. When they had scaled the Kendra's walls he stopped, unbuttoning his pants behind the drumstick tree.

'*Hath-gadi, hath-gadi,*' came a panting breath as Venkat's hand moved up and down in the region of his groin.

'Come on,' called Rahul, afraid someone might see them loitering.

Venkat ignored him, lost in the passions of his imagination, eyeballs gleaming insanely in the moonlight. Rahul watched the hand movements with growing excitement. Then a soft gasp escaped Venkat's lips and his body went limp. Still breathing heavily he straightened up and buttoned his pants. In the dorm, he fell on his bed and was lost to the world. But Rahul lay staring at the moonlight streaming onto his bed. In the morning his shorts felt sticky.

twelve

Honey-coloured eyes were Rahul's most striking feature. Turning golden in sunlight, the wide-set eyes gave him an air of innocence; the curly mop falling over his forehead added to his disarming looks. Years of street-life had made his hair red-edged but regular oiling at Bal Kendra corrected that. On the threshold of adolescence, Rahul cut as attractive a picture as any school-going boy.

Every few days a car or two would be parked in the Kendra's driveway. The visitors were usually couples in their thirties or forties. When they arrived, the child that had been matched with their preferences would be dolled up and put on display.

Rahul observed the visitors with trepidation. If they turned left from Sister Margaret's office, he could relax. If they turned right . . . Kajol was the most delightful of babies. The day he saw the girl in a red skirt with a tall, blond man getting out of a green Maruti Esteem, Rahul sensed something was going to happen. They were closeted with Sister Margaret for almost an hour. When they emerged, they turned right. Another hour passed. When eventually they returned, all three were smiling. 'She's so cute, I've fallen in love with her already,' he heard the girl say as she climbed into the car. Sister Angelina's tutoring had taught him a smattering of English and the woman's beatific expression confirmed his worst fears. His heart sank.

A few days later they came again, accompanied by a grey-haired woman in a pale blue sari, and went straight to Kajol's room where Sister Margaret was waiting. Again their faces were wreathed in smiles. Rahul couldn't stand it. The next morning he waylaid Sister Margaret. 'Has Kajol been adopted?' he asked bluntly.

She saw his anxious face. 'Pray for her, Rahul. She's growing fast,' she said kindly.

'Is that woman in the red skirt taking her?'

'What red skirt? The Connellys are interested in Kajol. But formalities have to be completed. Pray she finds a good home, Rahul.'

If at all Rahul prayed it would be to keep Kajol at Bal Kendra forever. But he had no power over Sister Margaret, let alone god. He had to think up his own devices. The next time he saw the Esteem in the driveway he hovered around. Sister Margaret saw him and called out. 'This is the boy who found her,' she said introducing him to the couple. 'Give him a token of appreciation when you take her.'

They wanted to ask a million questions. He answered sullenly with none of the panache that coloured his earlier narratives. Sister Margaret left him with them and returned to her office. Rahul took his chance. 'Baby legs burnt,' he began.

They nodded sympathetically. 'Poor dear has suffered so much. We're going to make it up to her by giving her the best,' sighed the woman, her eyes misty.

'ICU, one month,' Rahul continued, his chest constricting. 'Doctor said baby no live. Aparna-didi save

Meher Pestonji

her. Want to meet didi?'

They exchanged glances. 'I don't think we'll have the time,' said the blond man gently. 'Sandhya and I are returning to the States in a couple of weeks. There are so many papers to be processed. Sister Margaret's given us all the information on Tina.'

Rahul looked up sharply. 'Tina?'

The woman's features softened. 'We've decided to call her Tina.'

This was too much. They were giving Kajol a new identity already! He had to play his trump card. 'Burnt leg stay small, whole life. You know, no?'

'What?'

He drove in the poison. 'Doctor said leg not grow.'

The couple didn't come back for days.

Victory, he realized, was temporary. He was powerless to do more than delay the tryst with destiny. Sooner or later another couple would come and Kajol would go away. For her own good, he was told. But what about him?

The tenor of evenings in the garden changed. Instead of following Kajol as she chased butterflies or romped after a ball, he would clutch her close to his chest, cherishing the warmth of the cuddle, crooning fragments of Jitsu-Mitki. Some days they would just stand gazing at a statue of a mother and child in a stone grotto in a corner of the garden. Or he would carry her to the watchman's chair at the gate, sit her on his lap pretending they were waiting for a school bus that disgorged children into the waiting arms of mothers and maids. One day she would be like those children.

On one of his nightly escapades he looked up Karim-bhai at the barsati where he shared a bed in the 10 p.m. to 6 a.m. shift. The man who had vacated the bed was still sitting at its edge tying his shoelaces. Karim-bhai was waiting to change the sheets.

Karim-bhai's bed was on a veranda with two others, encased in stained mosquito nets. Beside it was a *matka* of drinking water with a long-handled *lota* which men dipped in to fill steel glasses or mugs. Most were migrants from states as far away as Assam, Kerala, Haryana, Tamil Nadu. The men earned by working shifts in factories, running petty businesses, offering freelance skills as house painters, masons, plumbers, electricians, but not enough to afford even a stamp-sized space in a city of mushrooming concrete towers. The owner of three rooms in a chawl capitalized on their need for space by renting beds in shifts.

'*Arre*! Munna-papa has become *ekdum chikna*!' exclaimed Karim-bhai, taking in Rahul's smart appearance.

Rahul smiled, suddenly shy. They were meeting after more than five months. 'I have a job now,' he said.

'*Wah*! First becomes a father, then gets a job . . . Where are you working?'

'At Kajol's centre.'

'*Shabhash*! Child gives father job! Why can't everyone do things *ulta-pulta*?

Rahul grinned happily, telling Karim-bhai about his new life. Karim-bhai listened, chuckling from time to time. Without the crocheted cap he wore outdoors, Karim-bhai looked unfamiliar. It seemed to belong on his head like an extension of his hair. But the embrace was warm as always.

'So, *bachcha* is turning over a new leaf,' said Karim-bhai jovially. 'In any case you can't steal anything from me here. All my things are locked in the trunk.'

'I came to meet you, chacha,' said Rahul, spotting the tin trunk under the bed. 'I've given up stealing.'

'Tell me another. Stealing is second nature to you.'

'I'm no more a thief than Bablu is a beggar. We play games. Like Lord Krishna.'

Karim-bhai's face clouded. 'Keep gods out of this, *bachcha*. These days religion is used to justify crimes worse than stealing. Have you heard what happened in Gujarat?'

Rahul shook his head. The middle-aged vendor's mood changed. He lapsed into silence. Rahul kept looking at him but the face before him was a stranger's. Capless, tense, devoid of the humour Rahul knew so well.

At last Karim-bhai emerged from his shell and looked directly at Rahul. 'I'm wondering how much to tell you,' he began softly. 'A child your age gets easily disturbed. He should not hear such things. But terrible things are happening. Hindus and Muslims are being goaded into hating each other . . .'

His voice trailed off. The shadow on his face deepened as he struggled with an inner world Rahul could not fathom. Then he spoke again. 'A wave of madness has swept over our country. It comes every few years. Hindus and Muslims go on a rampage killing each other, looting, raping, burning houses . . . And the police turn blind, deaf, dumb in another kind of madness. The insane inhumanity of indifference. The gods of every religion would be ashamed of the crimes committed in their names, of the criminals who pass off as their followers. That's why I say don't speak the name of god lightly.'

Rahul had never seen Karim-bhai in such a sombre mood. The fruit vendor he knew was playful and fun-loving. Something terrible must have happened. 'I may have stolen from you, chacha, but I will never, never hate you or hurt you,' he declared.

Karim-bhai kept looking at him. 'I hope that lasts,' he said softly.

'It will,' cried Rahul with youthful abandon. 'You are my friend, Bablu is my friend, Vicky is my friend and that's more important than anything else.' Karim-bhai began to smile.

The bus stopped behind the water tanker at the traffic lights. Rahul stared vacantly out of the window, impatient for it to move. He was late. If he didn't reach Chitra in half an hour the film would have started. Up ahead he saw a movement in the dark. A woman with a child astride her hip was unscrewing a tap at the rear of the tanker. As water gushed out she cupped her free hand and drank. Then she put her child's face to the water, urging it to drink. Luckily the light remained red. She turned off the tap, cupped her hand again and tapped at the window of a silver Mercedes.

Lights changed, traffic spurted forward. Rahul held his breath as the woman scurried to the side of the road. He jumped off the bus.

She squatted at the kerbside, visible only in flashes of headlights. He could see her form but not her face. A silhouette of two heads connected at the waist. The child broke free, trying to run. The mother grabbed its leg. It fell. It looked older than Kajol. Rahul couldn't tell whether it was a boy or a girl. As cars slowed at amber, stopped at red, the woman got up, extending her palm again. The film forgotten, Rahul stood on the opposite pavement, watching her.

This child was definitely not hired. Something in their body language communicated beyond words. The woman kept approaching cars and managed to collect a few coins till traffic thinned. Then she walked towards a cluster of huts at the far end of the road, pattering feet keeping pace behind her. Plucking up courage Rahul accosted her.

'Did you earn much, ma-ji?' he asked gently.

She swung around and picked up the child protectively. He was shocked to see how young she was. 'How does it concern you?' she snapped.

'I too have grown up in the streets,' he said simply.

She glanced at his clothes, incredulous. 'What do you want?'

He had no reply. 'Nothing,' he mumbled, reluctant to move away. The child was sucking its thumb, pulling at the mother's hair. The mother untangled its fist, smacked the offending hand lightly and immediately put it to her mouth, covering it with kissing sounds. The child lowered its head to the mother's shoulder. As Kajol did on his. Impulsively Rahul slipped a hand into his pocket and took out the fifty rupees he had kept for the film. Awkwardly he held it out. 'Get some food, for both of you,' he told the woman, embarrassed by his own gesture.

The woman kept looking at him quizzically. 'Why?' she asked.

'Because . . . because you are a mother,' he mumbled, tears stinging his eyes.

Night-time escapades were now regular for Rahul, most often with Bablu. They would see a film or go to the beach, tucking into their favourite snacks, with Rahul uncomplainingly footing the bill.

On a night windier than usual they found the beach flooded with bright lights. Petromax lanterns danced at the whim of the wind, shrinking and elongating shadows. Food stall owners enticed clients with catcalls that almost drowned the clanging of steel plates and spoons. A heady smell of onion, tamarind and coriander spiced the breeze. Rahul was hungry. He splurged on bhel and sevpuri followed by kulfi.

'Where do you get so much money, *hahn*?' said Bablu, eyeing him suspiciously even as he rubbed his stomach in satisfaction. As Rahul's face hardened, he hurriedly put an arm around him. 'You're lucky to have me help you spend it, yaar.' Rahul stifled his retort.

In the midst of the brightly lit area workers scurried around laying ramps on which a huge camera was mounted. A squat bald man barked orders into a megaphone as a boy with a clapper board waited for the shooting to begin.

'Sush or Aish, Sush or Aish,' speculated Bablu as they pressed through the crowd.

'Kajol! I want to see Kajol!'

'Don't you see enough of her?' came Bablu's scornful voice.

They wormed their way to the front as security men held off the crowd with lathis. At last a clean-shaven man stepped into the lighted arena followed by a stunning woman.

'Aamir Khan!'

'And Bipasha!'

Bablu clutched Rahul's shoulder, transfixed by the oomph girl. 'I dare you to talk to her,' he said defiantly, without shifting his gaze.

'If only she was closer . . .'

'I'll take you close. Get on my shoulders.'

Eagerly Rahul climbed on to Bablu's shoulders and Bablu ran forward. 'Hi, Aamir! Hi, Bipasha!' cried Rahul, waving wildly as security men chased. Aamir waved sportingly. Bipasha turned, smiled weakly and walked into a waiting car. A boy from the film crew stuck out his leg. The boys fell over, laughing. Rahul broke into the gyrating hip thrusts that had earned him an audience at the last party, then ran to the car and pressed his face against the glass.

'*Hato-hato-hato! Jao! Chale jao!* Never seen films, what?' shouted the director as he strode towards them.

'Films are *naqli*. These are *asli*.'

'Film stars are also human. They get scared of crowds at night.'

'We're not going to hurt her. We love her, we dream about her . . .'

'What else do you dream about?'

'Becoming rich and famous. Having lots of cars like Govinda. And a house with a hundred rooms.'

Bablu was looking at him with an incredulous expression. But the director looked amused. 'Why do you want a hundred rooms?' he asked.

'All big people have them. One room for sleeping, one room for eating, one room for cooking, one room for TV . . .' His voice faltered.

'Go on.'

'One room for mother, one for father, one for brother–sister . . .'

'That's eight rooms. You still have ninety-two more.'

'For all different women,' yelled someone from the crowd.

The director swung around. 'Oh yeah? Which of you

can have ninety women in a single night?' The crowd sniggered. 'That's only for dreams. There's a gap between dreams and reality, as between stars on screen and stars in life. On screen film stars spin dreams but in life they are as vulnerable as you and me.'

'Lecture-*baazi chhodo*! We want to see her!'

'Go see *Jism* at Lido.'

'We want to see her bo-dy . . .'

The director lost his flamboyance, peering uncertainly at the crowd pressing around the car. Swiftly he changed tack. 'Tch-tch-tch. You people are crazy about actor-actresses? They are workers like you! I'm the director, their boss. They have to do as I say. I say sit, they sit. I say stand, they stand. So who's the real hero? I am. What do you say, *tapori*s?'

He was standing in front of them, looking straight into their faces. Bablu burst into laughter. 'You? Who are you? Just some rich babu! Who wants to dream of an ugly fellow like you?'

The crowd laughed, the tension dissolved. People started drifting away. At the bus stop Bablu lost no time venting his spleen. 'Where do you get your big-big ideas? You are not a hero, understand. Once a *tapori*, always a *tapori*.'

Rahul got on the bus and left Bablu behind.

After the first night out with Venkat, Rahul had to contend with Venkat's constant pestering. To appease him Rahul took him to a film in the video parlours of Mankhurd, to addas where slum kids played *patta*. But Venkat had one insistent demand: he wanted to go back to the girls. Finally, Rahul relented.

Venkat kept up a nervous chatter all the way into town.

As they neared Shuklaji Street he kept fingering the twenty-rupee note in his pocket. He didn't take much time to choose a girl, walking up to a big-breasted one in a parrot-green salwaar-kameez. They disappeared behind the flimsy curtain.

On the return journey he was quiet. Rahul thought he was dozing. One day his needs too would be demanding. One day he too would visit girls, have his own woman . . . As the train pulled into Vashi he nudged Venkat awake. They caught the last bus, then tramped to Bal Kendra. Venkat scaled the wall before Rahul. Then Rahul heard him scream.

'Where's Rahul?' came Sister Margaret's voice as the bright beam of a torch scoured the top of the wall. Rahul cowered. He could hear skirmishes in the bush. Then an iron-like grip closed around his shoulder. 'He's here, madam,' came the watchman's voice. He was shoved in through the gate.

'Where have you been?' stormed Sister Margaret.

'We . . . we just went to have ice cream,' stuttered Venkat. Rahul nodded.

Sister Margaret knew she would never hear the truth. Ignoring Rahul she turned on Venkat. 'You've never broken bounds before. This boy is a bad influence.' Turning to Rahul, she added, 'Tomorrow you will move out of the boys' dorm. Anthony will keep an eye on you.'

A musky aroma permeated the air as strings of orange flowers interspersed with slender leaves adorned cars, buses, tempos and even humble handcarts. A basket of *torans* arrived at Bal Kendra. The most elaborate, with marigold semicircles framing tinsel balls, was hung over the main entrance. A smaller *toran* adorned Sister Margaret's office; simple ones were strung over the doors of each dormitory.

Dussehra, the festival of marigolds and mango leaves, reminded Rahul of Chandni. It had been ages since he had seen her or even thought of her. But the orange flowers stirred memories of her nimble fingers weaving intricate designs. Four nights later he managed to slip away earlier than usual and headed straight for the flower market. Only three flower stalls were open, selling aboli *venis* laced with silver tinsel. Other stalls did brisk business with shoppers in a festive mood running fingers over soft dupattas, eyeing piles of thick bedsheets, inspecting towels, belts, vests, briefs and bras pointed into peaks draped suggestively over clotheslines. Rahul strolled between stalls savouring the excitement of Diwali around the corner.

Then he spotted the cat atop a pile of crates, prowling around another. Rahul's eyes darted around. No Chandni, no grandmother. Only the furry feline. As he turned away in disappointment, a handkerchief fluttered against his face. It was clipped on a rotating wheel. One half had small floral hankies edged with yellow, blue, red and pink; the other had gents' handkerchiefs with blue, grey and brown borders. Rahul flicked the wheel playfully, converting it into a colourful fan. Abruptly he arrested its movement by grabbing a red-bordered hanky. Red for Kajol, he thought, then opted for blue. As he paid the vendor he looked for the cat again. It was no longer on the crates, not even on the cartons behind them. He looked over the flower stalls. No Chandni, no grandmother, no cat.

As in the old days, he ordered vada-pao, sniffing familiar fragrances as spicy potato batter entered hot oil. Just as he was about to bite into the vada he spotted her. She appeared as a shopper, not a vendor, wearing the yellow-green *ghaghra-choli* she had worn to the Don Bosco party, the *ghaghra* rising above her ankles, the *choli* tight with early breast-buds. She was with a woman who fondly held a ribbon from a stall against her hair. Overcome with shyness he slunk into the shadows, hoping nevertheless that she would see him. She did, slipping behind her mother and pointing in his direction. Her mother turned and smiled. Chandni skipped over. 'Seeing you after many days,' she began.

'I have a job now.' She made a face showing she was impressed. 'How's your leg?'

'It's been all right for ages.'

He didn't know what to say next. 'Here,' he said, thrusting the hanky towards her.

She looked startled. 'For me?'

He nodded. Her face turned radiant. She sniffed the hanky, grinned and ran back to her mother. Rahul felt elated.

The sudden cooling of the Connellys' interest in Kajol worried Sister Margaret. As the day of their departure neared, she called them up and was told they had changed their minds. A little probing had the mother-in-waiting haltingly confess they didn't have the courage to take on a child with a life-long handicap. Sister Margaret immediately put them in touch with Aparna who made them phone the doctor who'd treated Kajol. Fears abated, the Connellys lost no time pushing the adoption papers. But Sister Margaret was livid with Rahul. 'You ungrateful wretch! We're struggling to give you a future and you deprive an innocent child of one. How wicked can you get!' she stormed, her palm a stinging red from the uncharacteristic slap she had landed on his face.

'I . . . I want to keep Kajol,' he whimpered.

'Keep her? Can you feed her? Clothe her? Send her to school? Get real, Rahul. Give up your dream world! Life is tough.'

He had never seen her so angry. She went on raving, her words spinning around the room, bouncing off Rahul's eardrums without making contact with his brain. At last she sent for Anthony. 'You have lost your assistant,' she told him. 'Rahul will be leaving Bal Kendra tomorrow.'

Rahul whirled. He had not expected this. 'Wh-why? I . . . I'm sorry. . .' he blabbered in shock.

'My decision is final,' she said in a cold voice. 'Bal Kendra can't take any more risks for a delinquent boy.'

He gave up any attempt at listening. His future with Kajol had hit emptiness.

thirteen

On the surface the parting was unemotional. Sister Margaret summoned him to her office, settled his dues, including a cash gift from Kajol's new parents, and informed Sharan to expect him the next day.

'I'm sorry our experiment with you failed. You had such potential,' she said.

He looked at his feet knowing it was too late to plead, uncomfortable at the defeat in her eyes.

'Be careful with money,' she continued. 'If you had listened to me and saved it, it would have come in use now. In future save for rainy days.' With that she got up, indicating the meeting was over.

As the train gathered speed over Thane Creek Rahul realized he was not as unhappy to leave Bal Kendra as he had thought he would be. Without Kajol it held little attraction for him. A flock of birds, suspended in the loop of an air current, flapped wings in unison, moving neither backward nor forward, neither left nor right, as if connected by invisible links. As Rahul watched, one bird shot ahead, swerving to the left. The flock followed, a stray one lagging behind.

Though Rahul had missed Sharan he did not feel like returning. He had got used to sleeping on a bed. For half a day he sat at Vashi station, its height and granite no longer intimidating him. It had been nice to have a job. Surely he could get another? Work in a restaurant. Sweep-swab floors, clear tables, wash dishes. Udipi restaurants hired young boys like him. Shekhar had worked in one, so had Bablu.

But first he needed a roof over his head. Nearly two thousand rupees sat in his wallet. He was afraid of being pick-pocketed. He couldn't sleep on the station bench. Before night he had to find a safe place to keep his money and the four shirts, two shorts and one pair of pants he had been allowed to take. The only place he could think of was Karim-bhai's barsati. It was cheap and had beds. He reached to find Karim-bhai's bed occupied by someone who had covered himself from head to toe. Other beds on the veranda were also occupied. But two bunk beds along a wall of the dormitory were empty. There was also space on the floor.

Rahul approached the attendant to be told there was no vacancy among the veranda beds. The bunk beds were taken for the night but one was vacant in the morning shift, 6 a.m. to 2 p.m., and two in the afternoon shift, 2 p.m. to 10 p.m. The floor accommodated as many as would fit. Rahul checked in for the morning shift. It didn't solve his problem for the night but he could get Karim-bhai to keep his plastic bag in his trunk.

Then he went searching for Bablu. He found him under an overbridge between railway tracks where Salim and his gang played *jua*. He stood behind his friend, daylight making conspicuous the difference in cleanliness and clothes. Salim saw him first. 'Eh, *naqli*-papa. What are you doing here?'

'I've left Bal Kendra,' he said, as Bablu landed a delighted whack on his back.

'So are we to garland *naqli*-papa and welcome him back to Sharan?' asked Salim sarcastically, patting his chappals.

'I'm not coming back,' snapped Rahul. 'I've taken a bed in a barsati.'

'Why?' exclaimed Bablu, dismayed. 'Everyone comes back to Sharan.'

'He's got too many airs. Look at his clothes. Does he look like one of us?'

Salim's sneer sparked Rahul's adrenalin. 'You're right. I'm not going to remain *sadak chhaap* all my life. I'm going to make something of myself. Govinda began as a *kela-wallah*. Look where he is today. Remember Vinod, the *hamaal* at VT station? I saw him driving a Maruti.'

'Govinda could dance. Vinod can drive. What can you do, *chutiya*?' sneered Salim.

'I can sign my name, read a little and keep accounts now.'

Salim raised hands over his head in mock applause. 'I-can-sign-my-name-read-and-keep-accounts-now,' he mocked. 'Hero Number One *aya*. Like Amitabh Bachchan he's on his way to becoming *crorepati*. *Sawaal*: What is Rahul Kumar's *doosra naam*? *Jawaab*: Crorepati. *Lock kiya jaye*? *Hahn. Ban gaya*! Now Mr Rahul Kumar Crorepati, may we have your money?'

'*Chhod* yaar. What's wrong with improving yourself?'

'Go. Improve yourself. Just stay away from us.'

'I'm going. Come Bablu.'

Salim fixed Bablu with a hard stare. 'If you go with him, don't come back to Sharan,' he said nastily.

'Don't listen to him Bablu!' cried Rahul. 'Report him to Victor for threatening you!'

'Victor's term is over,' said Salim. 'I am *pradhan mantri* now, understood? Now scoot!'

'You? *Pradhan mantri*?' He whirled on Bablu but his friend reluctantly sat down with the card players. Rahul looked at him in disbelief. Slowly, he walked away.

He discovered he had grown tall when he didn't fit on his old bench. His knees felt cramped when they were bent for a while. His head pressed into the armrest. The cement felt cold and hard. Even the moon was unfriendly, rising after midnight like a sickle without a handle. Mosquitoes feasted on his face.

Groggy and grumpy, Rahul left the bench at the first streak of dawn and headed for the barsati. The previous occupant was still in the bathroom. Rahul moved aside his sheet, sprawled across the bed and fell asleep.

That afternoon he started the job-hunt, scouring restaurants. No one wanted another boy. Refusing to get dejected, Rahul tried restaurants further from Dadar station, only to meet the same response.

Two weeks passed. Funds dwindled. Each day set him back by over fifty rupees—paying for the barsati, food, bath and the late-night film necessary to minimize time on the bench. In desperation he bought a lottery ticket and gave it to Chandni for luck.

'How do you know I won't run away with your money if you win?' she teased.

'I'll catch your grandmother.'

'I'll take her with me!'

'Gimme back my ticket.'

'I won't! It's mine now!'

He returned to grabbing seats on long-distance trains but found himself up against an aggressive new gang defending its turf. He offered to carry luggage for less than the normal fee, but red-shirted porters pushed him away, brandishing their badges before passengers. He could no longer get away with filching. He was too tall to be inconspicuous. Even Karim-bhai stopped giving him free fruit. He had joined the ranks of workers. He had savings. He had entered the adult world.

'Let's start a *dhanda*,' Rahul told Bablu who had sneaked away from Salim's gang to meet Rahul at the vada-pao stall.

'What business?'

'I'll buy bananas wholesale. You sell them and we'll share the profits.'

'Where will you buy wholesale?'

'The wholesale market at Vashi isn't far from Bal Kendra.'

'Where will I sell them?'

'At the station.'

'Salim would kill me!'

'Dadar isn't the only station. You could set up a stall at Kurla, Mahim, Bandra . . .'

'And pay *haftas*. Have you become such a gentleman to forget all that?'

Rahul's dream-bubble imploded. 'I need a job, Bablu,' he said despondently.

'Jobs don't grow on trees waiting to be plucked like fruit,' replied Bablu. 'Be sensible and return to Sharan.'

'With Salim in charge? Never.'

The barsati housed several job seekers as desperate as he. Every week a few lost their toehold on respectability for defaulting on charges. Rahul panicked as he saw them leave, sentenced to street life. What if he had to follow?

'If you knew tailoring I could have helped you,' said Girish, who occupied the bed next to Rahul's, scratching his forehead with the pencil stub he kept tucked behind his right ear. 'What use is reading-writing if it doesn't help you earn?'

'Sister was going to send me to school,' he said ruefully.

'All these people have been to school,' said Girish, sweeping a hand around the barsati. 'Standard six, standard eight. Even ten and twelve. What use is it? Because I can stitch I earn even if I don't have a job.'

Girish had hired a corner of the barsati for his sewing machine. Rahul would awake to the rhythmic khus-khus-khus of machine pedals. Reams of cloth sat in piles on the floor. Girish was stitching curtains for a hotel. When two sets were ready he offered to pay Rahul for delivering them.

The Gateway Hotel was on the sixth floor of a building without a lift. Carrying the large parcel, Rahul staggered up steep stairs. At last he was facing the receptionist. 'Change the curtains in room number five before the occupant returns,' instructed the receptionist. 'Hurry.'

Rahul tried to look nonchalant as he was ushered into the room and the door hastily shut behind him. He examined the curtains at the window. They moved left, they moved right. He had no idea how to bring them down. He tugged. Something made a clicking sound. But the curtains stayed firmly in place.

Four pink floral curtains had to be hung. A pair at each window. Rahul spread them out on the bed, admiring the pattern. Pulling a chair to the window he slung the new curtains over the old. They were short; the old ones formed a jagged border at the bottom, with mismatched colours.

Trying to look nonchalant, Rahul slunk along a narrow corridor, slipping into a door left slightly ajar. He found himself at the head of a spiral staircase running parallel to drainage pipes and ran down, relieved at avoiding the receptionist.

fourteen

R ahul wandered out of the narrow gully and found himself on a wide road with a row of antique shops in buildings whose awnings shaded the pavement. Banaras brocades, Kashmir shawls and carpets, Tibetan tankhas, silver jewellery with semi-precious stones. As Rahul stared in fascination, a shopkeeper shouted, '*Chale jao! Hath mat lagao!*'

Before him was the imposing stone façade of the Taj Mahal Hotel. A tempo was disgorging frozen carcasses into its innards as three uniformed men chatted with the driver. If the rear entrance is so imposing, what will the front be like, he wondered, strolling down a shaded portico where two snot-nosed kids squatted with a cracked plastic mug, oblivious of their imperious shelter. All at once he found himself confronting the sea.

He couldn't decide which was more beautiful, the monument or its setting. He alternated his gaze between the majestic Gateway of India on a stone pier and the harbour with misty mountains beyond. The Gateway's magnificent arches were bordered by intricately carved spiral minarets. A cobbled walkway all around was fringed by bobbing boats beyond which ocean liners glided silently, fluffy clouds keeping pace with their imperceptible movement.

The Taj forgotten, Rahul ambled down the walkway, past vendors of peanuts and gram, wafers and candy floss, tourist caps, guide books and postcards, and sat on the stone ledge carved into seats around the Gateway. The sculpted stone was smooth and rough at the same time, like the bark of some trees. Below him water rose and fell without breaking into waves. The undulating movement fascinated him. The seafronts he was familiar with—Chowpatty, Mahalaxmi, Juhu—had limitless horizons. Mountains encasing the harbour defined space, made it intimate, gave him a sense of belonging.

A boat sidled up to the stone steps of the jetty. A boatman slipped a rope into a stone ring embedded in the ground, and pulled. The boat swayed wildly, steadied, drew close. Fastening the rope, the man began enticing passengers for joy rides. This will be the next adventure with Bablu, decided Rahul, regretting that his friend was not with him.

At five in the evening the place was teeming. Chattering groups, babies in prams wheeled by ayahs, kids playing ball, hopscotch, with balloons, and ice cream vendors doing brisk business. Rahul was surprised at the number of foreigners, with fair skin and dark, with chinky eyes and blue. He eyed them warily. One of their tribe had taken Kajol.

'*Ek rupaiya mein dekho! Ek rupaiya mein dekho!*' The voice was shrill and penetrating. The man stood behind a long brass cylinder pointed towards the sea. People queued up to peer in. Rahul's curiosity was aroused. What was inside this cylinder? He waited for the crowd to thin before offering his rupee. He put his eye to the glass and found himself transported to a ship, within touching distance of a sailor sitting cross-legged on the deck, thick ropes coiled at his side. Delighted, he turned the telescope towards a lighthouse. The image blurred. Before the attendant could re-focus Rahul swung it towards another ship where a crane was lifting a container as big as a house. Then his time was up.

His perch along the ledge had been taken by a fat woman in a yellow sari. He approached a sandwich vendor, changed his mind and bought peanuts. A grey-haired woman was scattering grain among waddling pigeons between the Gateway and the Taj. Rahul strolled through the gaggle, enjoying the breeze from fluttering wings. He liked the feel of salt air against his skin, the wind blowing the curly mop away from his face, even the acrid smell of decaying fish when the tide went out. Impulsively he decided to skip his nightly film and stay late at this charming venue.

As he walked along the pier, the lights came on. They were not ordinary street lights. A pair of round globes on ornate poles emitted a glow that softened darkness. Lights that created atmosphere. Lights that held secrets, concealing and revealing at the same time. And in the sea, ships became clusters of stars competing with those in the sky.

The growls in his stomach were becoming insistent. Fragrant aromas announced the proximity of a restaurant. He walked into Cafe Baghdadi. Among its assortment of diners, he shared a table with a bearded foreigner who smiled at him. Rahul concentrated on his biryani with a double-jointed leg of chicken. Thirty-five rupees would make a dent in his pocket but he didn't care. The special place made it a special day and he was feeling reckless.

An unusual number of solitary women were hanging around when he emerged. But while the gaudy women at

Shuklaji Street swung arms flirtatiously and leered at men, these looked stoic, morose, slinking into shadows from which flashed pouting red mouths and gleaming teeth. Rahul felt repulsed.

Stretching out on the stone ledge Rahul cushioned his head in his hands. Light from a half moon pierced the pale mist that shielded stars. The rhythmic whoosh of waves against the pier soothed him. As his eyelids drooped, he heard a woman's voice rasping, 'Dance *karne ka sau rupaiya. Aur kuch chahiye to aur dena padega.*' But he was floating away.

When orange penetrated his eyelids he opened his eyes to a sun balanced precariously on a minaret. Without moving he watched them part. Till he heard a fart. The bearded foreigner was relieving himself in a corner. He was outraged. This was not a rail track. This place was special. Foreigners are devils, he thought, resolving to keep away.

Karim-bhai put a damper on his spirits. He had taken his wife and son to the Gateway when they came to Bombay. 'It's only nice to visit,' he said tartly. 'People like us must know where we belong. If we go to places meant for *bade log* we only get into trouble.'

Karim-bhai was spouting too many homilies these days, thought Rahul. How was he to know where he belonged? Certainly not in his village. Not Bal Kendra. Not even within the porous walls of Sharan. Was he to accept street life as his destiny for fear of crossing lines? Govinda had crossed over, and Vinod was driving a Maruti. Even the fixed lines of rail tracks led to exciting destinations.

Rahul was not afraid of trouble. He had got in and out of it ever since he could remember. Without getting into trouble he would never have got into Bal Kendra. And without getting thrown out he would never have discovered Apollo Bunder. Sensing that good times were inextricably coupled with bad ones, Rahul shrugged off Karim-bhai's pessimism.

'You call this sea? It's more like a lake,' said Bablu, unimpressed with the Gateway after Rahul's glowing descriptions. 'A real sea meets the sky.'

'That's all flat and boring. Look at the mountains, ships, pigeons.'

'You're getting too many airs. Go stay at Taj Mahal Hotel.'

'I'll show you something else,' said Rahul, steering Bablu towards the telescope. But Bablu was in no mood to be appeased.

'Just a gimmick, yaar,' he sneered, skipping down the stone steps of the jetty and jumping into a boat. As the boat took off, songs from *Monsoon Wedding* drowned out the lapping of waves. Rahul dropped a hand over the side, dragging it through an oil slick in the water. Cupping his fingers he splashed water over Bablu's head. '*Chhod* yaar,' cried Bablu, brushing droplets off his Ganguly shirt. 'The water's dirty!'

Rahul raised eyebrows in mock surprise. 'What's wrong with dirt?' he lisped.

Their eyes met, palms slapped, and the boys dissolved into roars of laughter, frightening a seagull that was hovering alongside. It squawked and soared into the sky, abandoning their boat.

'You're new.'

'Tch . . . I've been here four-five times.'

'I've seen you. But you don't talk to anyone.'

'I don't know anyone.'

'Come with me. We're all *sadak chhaap*. We live behind Radio Club.'

Rahul felt miffed at being called *sadak chhaap*. He liked to believe he had left the stamp of the streets behind. But this boy, who introduced himself as Dinesh, had identified him.

He followed Dinesh down Apollo Bunder, past Radio Club, whose pier also protruded into the sea, into a lane where plastic sheets were slung over a wall on one side and stretched over bamboo poles on the other to erect a shanty. Underneath, a boy was stirring a large aluminium *dekchi* while another dealt a pack of cards to imaginary players, on ground strewn with cigarette butts.

'Hey Zakhir, what's for lunch?' called Dinesh.

'Crab curry. With coconut, beans, tomatoes.'

'Not again!'

Dinesh turned to Rahul. 'Every day at low tide Zakhir and Arvind go down to the rocks and trap crabs. How many crabs did you get today?'

'Five, but two are very small.'

'Can we feed a guest?'

'No-no, don't bother,' said Rahul shyly.

'You can pay for what you eat,' replied Dinesh. 'Hey Zakhir, can we feed . . . what's your name?'

'Rahul.'

'Can we feed Rahul?'

'If he buys us bread.'

Dinesh turned to Rahul, raising his eyebrows. Rahul nodded. They went down a back lane dominated by dhobis. Sheets, towels, clothing flapped on clotheslines as men in tiny rooms thumped hot irons, sweat dripping over washed clothes. Tucked into a stairway was a glass counter for eggs, bread, milk, soft drinks, cigarettes. Rahul paid ten rupees for three *ladi*s.

'Where are you from?' asked Zakhir as Rahul dipped bread into the crab curry.

'A village near Raipur,' replied Rahul. The curry was delicious. He wondered why Dinesh had grumbled. He ate with Dinesh and Zakhir while the card player waited for a plate.

'How old are you?'

Rahul shrugged. 'Twelve, thirteen. . .'

'How long have you been in Bombay?'

'Five-six years.'

'So you're not new. Where do you live?'

'I was at Dadar . . . then Vashi. I had a job at Vashi. Helper to a mali.'

'Irfan also has a job. In a hotel. But he lives with us.'

'And brings vegetables,' grinned Dinesh with a wink. Arvind was still dealing cards to an invisible circle, gathering them up, shuffling, dealing again.

'Irfan is my brother,' said Zakhir quietly. 'We came together from Azamgarh one year ago. We send money to our mother.'

'If I go to my father I pretend to have no money. He takes it away,' said Dinesh.

'My father died,' said Rahul. 'My mother's new man beat me up.'

'Everywhere same story,' Arvind piped in, suddenly coming alive. 'Even my father got a new woman. She pressed my hand on hot-hot tawa. Also threw a lighted match on me. See?' He lowered his shirt, exhibiting a red

Meher Pestonji

welt on the shoulder. Rahul shuddered.

'Why did you leave your job?' asked Zakhir.

Rahul took his time crunching a crisp crab shell. Instinctively he knew that mentioning Kajol would be a mistake. 'I was caught stealing,' he said at last. That won instant approval.

'What are your plans now?' He shrugged. 'Okay, Rahul. You can stay with us. We can teach you tourist business. Money comes, money goes, like tourists. All you need is some words of English, Arabic, French, Italian . . .'

He did not want to become *sadak chhaap* again. But what was this tourist business?

'I'll come when I can,' he said, wiping the last traces of curry with bread.

'If you want to learn, you have to hang around,' advised Dinesh.

Rahul had already decided that's what he would do.

'She's dead.'

'Who?'

Rahul was surprised to find Karim-bhai at the barsati instead of the fruit stall at midday. His face was a grey wall as he stared stonily out of the window.

'My sister.'

'Was she ill?'

Karim-bhai shook his head.

'What happened?'

The wall remained dense. Rahul sat beside him, looking silently at the clenched hands in Karim-bhai's lap.

'Remember I told you about the riots in Gujarat?' came a soft voice just as Rahul was contemplating whether it might be better to leave.

'That was weeks ago.'

'She suffered these many weeks.' The chink in the walled face closed. Rahul fidgeted uncomfortably. He had no idea how to deal with grief.

Abruptly the crack widened. Pain flowed freely from the gaping gash. Words tumbled out haltingly, each chiselled away from a mass of seething emotions. In a staccato voice Karim-bhai told Rahul how his sister had been raped by three men from his village; how, afterwards, her private parts had been stuffed with chilli powder, how she had been left screaming, in an open field. She was found unconscious three days later and taken to a hospital, but the infection had spread. She lay there, writhing and screaming till at last she died. Rahul barely comprehended what he was told. But he sensed Karim-bhai's helpless anger combined with grief. An anger that could explode on innocent targets like himself, or dissipate into despair.

'Why didn't you tell me earlier?' he asked for want of anything else to say.

'Because you're a *bachcha*. Children shouldn't hear such things.' He paused a long time, repeatedly clearing his throat as he struggled with his emotions. 'Why do such things happen?' he continued at last. 'For religion? That would be a disgrace. No god—Muslim or Hindu, Christian or Sikh—will forgive criminals and murderers. Their sins will come back on their heads. Believe me, *bachcha*, those who make others suffer will burn in hells of their own making.'

Rahul was shaken by Karim-bhai's passion. He had never thought about god or death. To encounter both together was overwhelming.

When Karim-bhai spoke again his face was calm but his voice betrayed bitterness. 'I pray five times a day at the appointed hour,' he said, as if to himself. 'But what use has it been? Why doesn't Allah protect his followers, turn his wrath on those who are butchering us?' Tears were running into the black beard, remaining suspended, dropping onto his kurta when the jaw moved. He wiped his chin on his sleeve and turned to look at Rahul. 'Shall I go to pray today?' he asked in a voice as simple as a child's. 'What can I honestly say to Allah on a day like this?'

When he spoke again, his voice was flat, like a balloon from which air has escaped. 'Tell me Rahul, what should I say when I pray? Should I get angry with Allah for failing my poor sister? Or should I thank him for protecting my wife and son, saving them from these devils? What should I say to Allah, Rahul? What can I honestly say?'

Rahul couldn't bear it any more. He flung himself on the sobbing Karim-bhai's chest for just a moment. Then he fled. After a long time he found himself in the park with the swings, deliriously recreating Karim-bhai's images. Chilli powder inflamed the tiniest of cuts. He knew that well. To have it stuffed up a sensitive part of the body . . . He shuddered.

The swaying movement of the swing allowed thoughts to settle like grains in a bottle. A puddle of muddy water filled the hollow below the swing. Each time the swing rose, a sliver of moon raced under Rahul's feet. He spat into the puddle. The moon trembled into ripples, then regained form, untouched by the insult to its reflection.

He knew he was a Hindu. Sister Margaret had decided that on the basis of his name. He liked participating in *arti*s with tinkling bells and dancing flames, but his visits to the Hanuman temple were more for the music than for any god. He enjoyed clapping to the pundit's chants, swaying till the rhythm reached a crescendo. After the *arti* he felt exhilarated, as if some nebulous energy had permeated him.

Sister Margaret's way of praying was different. Each morning he had seen her go to the grotto in the garden, to the statues of Mother Mary and Jesus. An outcropping of round stones was hollowed into a bowl for water. Sister Margaret would dip her right hand in the water, make the sign of the cross, and light a candle before the mother and child. Then she would kneel and shut her eyes, a rosary of black beads passing between her fingers. Rahul wondered what she was thinking as she took the position of abject submission before her deity.

He had also seen Karim-bhai prostrate himself on his prayer mat. At the masjid he would be among dozens of devotees prostrating in straight lines as a maulana intoned incomprehensible words. They would stand, lift arms, change direction and prostrate again as Rahul watched the ritual from outside, fascinated at how so many became one in worship.

Kajol? Was she to be taken as Hindu because he had given her a Hindu name? What if her parents had been Muslim? What if her adoptive parents brought her up as a Christian? Did it matter as long as she grew up healthy and cared for?

Street lights were brighter than the thin slice of moon, more inviting. Rahul left the swing and sauntered towards them. He was in no mood for his nightly film, in no mood for the barsati, too restless to sleep. Aimlessly he let his feet carry him in and out of the station, past Kajol's bench. The crescent was a catty smile in the sky. A vague apprehension was clouding his head. Would Karim-bhai stay friendly with him, a Hindu, after this? Would his affection for Rahul dissolve? The thought was frightening. Bablu and Karim-bhai were the pillars of his life. If he lost one, he would feel as lame as Gopi.

For three days he stayed away from the barsati, glad that he had met Dinesh's group. Each night he would come to the Gateway after his film and be up early the next morning. The rest of the day was spent learning the tourist trade.

Sadak Chhaap

'Hullo!' 'Good morning. How are you?' '*Bonsoir*. You like India?' he heard Dinesh calling as he followed a tourist in bermudas. 'Want hotel? I show you good, cheap, clean.' Or, 'You wearing too good clothes, sir. You want good hotel, no? Best for best price I can show.' And 'Want to see Elephanta? Mombadevi temple? Hanging Gardens? I arrange boat, taxi . . .'

After a bit of simulated wrangling Rahul would see Dinesh climb into Shankar's cab with a wink and a thumbs-up sign. For his efforts he received tips from tourists, commissions from hotels, tourist shops and even from Shankar. After a week Rahul was ready to try on his own. He was eager to earn. The first two foreigners brushed him aside. The next one responded with a smile, asking for directions to the post office. Rahul told the young man, 'I show you.'

'Thank you. Where'd you learn English?' asked the friendly foreigner as they walked along the Apollo Bunder pier.

'Friends,' replied Rahul.

'Not in school?'

Rahul shook his head. 'Not gone school.'

'You've never been to school but speak a foreign language. Gee, that's wunnerful. Where'd your friends learn English?' Rahul shrugged. He spotted Dinesh and Arvind grinning. He ignored them. 'Where are your parents?'

'Mother, sister in village,' replied Rahul. 'Father dead.'

'Who do you live with?'

'Friends. On footpath.'

'A young boy alone in the streets of Bombay speaking a foreign language. That's amazing,' said the foreigner, sounding genuinely impressed. 'My students don't even speak one language correctly.'

He stopped to open his bag and take out a camera. 'Can I take your photograph?' he asked, framing Rahul against the backdrop of the Gateway. Rahul saw Dinesh rubbing a thumb over fingers, urging Rahul to ask for money. 'What's your name?' asked the foreigner as he took out a diary.

'Rahul.'

'Okay, Ra-ul, I'm a schoolteacher from Cincinnati in America. You've heard of the United States?' Did this foreigner take him for a fool? 'Don't let anyone put you down, Ra-ul,' he continued. 'You're smarter than the kids I teach. They couldn't survive in the street for a day, leave alone speak a foreign language. I'm going to show them your photograph.'

They had reached the post office. Dinesh was gesticulating wildly to ask for money before it was too late. 'Pepsi?' said Rahul hesitantly, looking down at his feet.

'I can do better than that,' smiled the foreigner, taking out his wallet. 'How much does lunch cost?'

'Fifty,' said Rahul, thinking of biryani at Baghdadi.

'Have two meals on me,' said the foreigner, waving him away.

He was exultant. He had earned one hundred rupees!

Dinesh and Arvind were dancing around him. '*Goli! Kali goli!*' they cried.

He looked at them warily. His savings had dwindled. He had to pay for his barsati. He had to fight becoming a *sadak chhaap*. He would have to hide his earnings.

sixteen

'Salaam walequm.'
'Walequm salaam. *Eisht abgha*?'
'Can I help you?'
'No.'

Rahul did not give up. He had been told Arabs were the most lucrative of tourists. He had to stick around.

'You want hotel? Very good hotel I can show.'
'I have a hotel.'
'I can take to best shops. Buy for wife, children.'
'I'm busy. Get lost!' snapped the Arab, flinging a crumpled note at Rahul.

As Rahul bent to pick it up he noticed the Arab's shoes. 'Polish sir? Shoes need polish?'

The Arab looked down. The polish did seem dull. 'I have an appointment. Come to my hotel at four o'clock.'

'Yes, sir. *Shukran*. I come at four.'

At the hotel the Arab had three pairs of shoes lined up for polishing. 'How much will it cost?' he asked, taking out his wallet.

'Hundred rupees each, sir,' replied Rahul. He could have taken all three for a hundred and still made a profit, but this was the price Dinesh had suggested.

'Isn't that too much?' asked the Arab uncertainly.

Rahul gulped. 'I will tell polish-wallah to do for less, sir,' he said, picking up the shoes before the Arab changed his mind.

'India's getting too expensive,' he muttered, and handed Rahul three hundred rupees. 'If you save money, keep it. You're not getting any more.'

Arabs were there to be fleeced. They paid ten times more than actual costs. While an Indian family paid twenty-five or thirty rupees for a *ghoda-gadi* ride, Arabs would be charged two or three hundred. It was the same for postcards, silk scarves, toys, balloons. Arabs had too much money, too little education, not enough confidence to question even when they suspected something was wrong.

'Arabs for money, *firangs* for fun,' smirked Dinesh, showing off a T-shirt gifted by a tourist with 'CK' embossed on its back. Rahul's eyes gleamed as Dinesh bragged about the ice cream, Pepsi and Kit-Kat treats he had received.

As the days went by, Rahul started scouring white faces for hints of naivety. One day he ran into a young woman, blonde, petite, pretty. She was climbing the stone steps of the jetty, returning from Elephanta Caves when he first saw her, looking wan under sunburnt skin. He approached her with his usual hello-you-want-hotel line to find her mouth contracting in a sob. 'Another thief,' she mumbled, brushing him away.

'Sorry, ma'am?'

'I don't want anything. Leave me alone.'

'You want good hotel?' he persisted, looking at her backpack.

'I don't want a hotel. Go away! Fuck off!' she snarled, raising her voice.

He backed off but kept watching her. She looked barely

a few years older than he and on the verge of tears. She took a few uncertain steps to the right, turned back towards the Taj, turned again and stood in front of the Gateway, looking at its arches. Putting her rucksack on the ledge she started rummaging in it, getting more and more frantic because she couldn't find what she was looking for. Rahul plucked up courage to approach her again.

'Lost something ma'am?' he asked tentatively.

She looked exasperated. 'My passport, money, credit cards, everything. You won't get anything from me, okay.'

'Go to consulate, ma'am,' he ventured tentatively, hoping Dinesh's briefing was right.

'How do I get there without money?' she snapped.

'My friend, taxi driver. You pay later.'

Her hostility dissipated. 'Is . . . is that possible?' His heart lurched as he saw anxiety lines leave her face.

A few hours later she was settling into a hotel recommended by Rahul. Her name was Karen. She was still a student, travelling for a year before joining university. While her boyfriend went trekking in Nepal she had decided to work with an NGO that helped children of prostitutes. She showed him a paper with an address. 'Can your taxi driver friend take me there?' she asked. 'I'm told it's not safe to go alone.'

'I'll come with you, ma'am,' he volunteered. She looked relieved. The next day he waited in the cab with an amused Shankar for two hours. Shankar, he discovered, had also grown up in the streets. He too had taken tourists around. In a few years he had saved enough for a second-hand car and converted it into a taxi.

'So I can save and buy a taxi?' asked Rahul, impressed.

'Only if you don't waste money on charas and ganja.'

He was getting to like charas a bit too much. It made him feel light, woozy, relaxed. After a joint at Apollo Bunder he would feel the breeze sweep him into clouds. Floating like a kite on a string. Maybe he could have a little charas and also save. Hadn't he started saving with Karim-bhai already?

'I'm going to become a taxi driver,' he told Bablu when they met.

'Which lion did you kill after becoming a cycle driver that anyone is going to let you drive a taxi?' sneered Bablu.

'I'm going to buy my own taxi.'

'Give up your *faltu* dreams and get real!' exclaimed Bablu. 'Come back to Sharan if you know what's good for you.'

'Never. Tourist business is good. I've already . . .' he stopped. Bablu knew nothing of his savings. Rahul hadn't told him, afraid he would become more demanding. Rahul did the spending on all their outings but there was a limit to the price he was prepared to pay for friendship.

After the first day, Karen didn't take Rahul to the red-light area again. They would meet at Apollo late at night. Sometimes she would buy him popcorn or chips and sit beside him chatting. She often asked about his family, showing him photographs of her parents with a big black dog, of her brother with a red-striped beach ball.

'Describe your mother for me,' she said since he had no photographs. 'Is she fat, thin, tall, short?'

'Thin.'

'And her face? What's her face like?'

A haze, he wanted to say. Too far in the past. Struggling with memory he hit upon two salient features. 'She had long nose. And red eyes.'

'Red eyes? Why? Did she cry a lot?'

'Red eyes from cooking.'

'Oh. What did she cook on? Coal?'

'Sticks and *gobar*.'

'Sticks and what?'

'*Gobar*. Cow shit. Sister and I collect from field. Dry in sun. Ma make fire with *gobar*, sticks and little kerosene. Kerosene expensive.'

Karen looked aghast as she digested this. 'You collected shit to help your mother! You poor child!' she exclaimed involuntarily.

He didn't see why she was so upset. He picked up cow dung only after it dried into cakes. His mother spread it over the floor to cool their hut and keep away mosquitoes. 'Cow is holy animal in India,' he ventured.

'I know. But touching its shit . . .' She shuddered.

To change the subject he asked, 'What you do with children of bad women?'

She looked up sharply. 'They aren't bad women, Rahul. It's just that their way of earning money is with their bodies. But sex workers want their children to have a better life, not end up sex workers like themselves. This NGO keeps children in a crèche while mothers work, sends children to school, conducts HIV tests . . .'

'But what you do?' he wanted to know.

'I? I thought I could help children with school work. Then I found most go to Hindi or Marathi schools, so there's a language problem. For the first few days I just hung around observing. Then a social worker asked me to catalogue the video films in their library. I guess I'm learning more than contributing.'

'You like poor, dirty children?'

'They're full of beans!' She laughed as she saw his confused expression and patted his arm affectionately. 'Look at you, Rahul. You're a survivor. You've been through ups and downs but you've come through. You should see street kids in the West. They're on drugs, on alcohol. They don't have half your spirit. You kids are in the street because of poverty. You can go home whenever you want. They are in the street because their families don't want them. If they were to go home their parents would slam the door in their faces.'

Could he go home, he wondered. What home? He had no idea where his mother would be after all these years. She too might slam the door in his face—if she had a door. Karen was too starry-eyed about India.

Before returning home, Karen presented him a pair of sunglasses. 'Because you work in the sun and I don't want you to have red eyes like your mother,' she said. Delighted, he put them on, rose-tinting his vision of the world. The glasses sealed his infatuation with Karen for months. He rode with her to the airport in Shankar's cab.

For the return ride Shankar was determined to pick up an Arab. He deftly steered the cab to a strategic position, letting others pass towards the pre-paid counter. The traffic cop whistled. Shankar pretended to fumble at the dashboard. 'Looking for PUC certificate, sa'ab,' he said.

As a man in a black *jalabeya* emerged from the departure lounge Shankar zoomed up. He was with a woman, three children and a heavily laden luggage trolley. The woman was plump with a turquoise scarf covering her hair. Her youngest child lay across her shoulder sucking a thumb. While Shankar loaded the cab, Rahul stood behind, smiling at the child. He felt a tug above his knee. The second child was speaking Arabic. He touched her lightly on the cheek, gesturing he didn't understand. The man showed Shankar a card with the name of a hotel.

'Sea Bird Hotel is in Colaba,' said Shankar, winking at Rahul. The card read Wadala.

Only the man spoke English. He told them they had brought the youngest son for treatment. The boy had a perpetual cough for which they wanted to consult the best doctor in Bombay.

'I know very good doctor, sir,' said Shankar. 'I can take you.'

The man hesitated, spoke to his wife in Arabic. Rahul could see them confabulating in the rear-view mirror. 'Is he far from hotel?' asked the man.

'Lady doctor it is, sir. Very good. Child specialist.'

Again the Arab translated for his wife. She seemed to approve. 'Can you make appointment?' asked the Arab.

Shankar pulled up at Sea King Hotel, known for hefty commissions. He spoke to the receptionist in Hindi. The family was ushered into a large comfortable room. The woman put the sleeping child on the bed and looked around, pleased. The man thrust a handful of notes into the receptionist's hand. After their door shut, the receptionist handed some to Shankar. Rahul got his commission for introducing him to Karen.

By the time Rahul reached Radio Club the next day Shankar had left three messages for him. The Arab family wanted him to look after the two children while they were with the doctor. He would be paid five hundred rupees for the day. 'Now you will see real money,' said Shankar conspiratorially. 'But one hundred is my commission.'

Dr Nupur Modi's office was sleek, with sunmica panelling, a bowl of plastic flowers on the centre table and an assortment of English and Arabic publications in a magazine rack. The mother looked tense, an arm protectively around the sick child. Rahul carried the youngest as he had carried Kajol ages ago. The second child was hyperactive, tossing magazines, plucking plastic flowers, running up and down the corridor.

At last they were called in. Nupur Modi spoke fluent Arabic. She examined the sick child, talking to the couple, writing on a notepad. The child was sent for blood, urine and sputum tests. They were to return with reports. As they prepared to leave, the doctor's eye fell on the child in Rahul's arms. She beckoned to Rahul, shone a torch into the child's eyes, ears, throat, her expression turning grave. The parents grew alarmed. They rattled off in Arabic again. Rahul saw Nupur Modi write another prescription.

'This is just the beginning,' exulted Shankar. 'The pathology lab also gives commissions. In the next week we'll make a packet.'

'What's wrong with the small child?' asked Rahul.

'Nothing. Modi's smart. She'll charge five hundred for vitamin injections and keep getting her fees as well.'

'But if there's nothing wrong with the child . . .'

'So what? Vitamins will make it strong.'

Nine days later, after dropping the family to the airport, Shankar went to collect his commission. Nupur Modi tried to haggle. 'Ten thousand is a lot of money,' she said. 'Be satisfied with five.'

Shankar looked at her disdainfully. 'You're not the only doctor in Colaba. All my patients will go to Aziz Sheikh.'

She paid up without another word. Rahul was content

121   *Sadak Chhaap*

with his babysitting fees. But he made a decision: he would not fleece sick people. Somehow that seemed wrong.

'Arabs are fools,' he told Chandni a few days later. 'It's easy to make money from them.'

'Who are Arabs?'

'People from Dubai, Muscat, Saudi. Fat men wearing burkhas like women with hoods around their heads, like this.' He took off Karen's glasses and made a funny face, puffing out his cheeks and covering his head with a plastic wrapper to amuse her.

A vendor slipped sliced limes into a squeezer and pressed down, dripping juice into one glass, then another, topping them up with dubious-looking water. Holding an empty glass rim to rim with the full ones, he inverted them back and forth to mix the juice, then handed them to Rahul.

'Where's the ice?' The vendor lobbed in a lump of ice and Rahul held out a glass to Chandni.

'Saudi is good for making money,' she said. 'My mother works in Saudi.' He nodded. But her next sentence knocked him cold. 'She is finding a boy for me.'

'A boy?'

She nodded. 'I'm nearly fifteen. Nani-ma said it's not safe for a girl to be alone after a certain age. She's not going to live forever.' She kept looking at him.

He was flummoxed. He fumbled. He didn't know what to say. 'It's . . . it's too soon. We're . . . you're too young . . .' he stammered.

She nodded sadly. 'It's not safe for girls to be alone,' she repeated.

He downed his juice in a gulp and asked for another. The vendor dipped the glass in a pink plastic bucket, rinsed it by pouring water from shoulder height back into the bucket, then squeezed another lime into it.

'Is there a boy?' he managed to ask.

She nodded again. 'Lives in a pukka house with TV. My mother knows his mother.'

'So you'll be leaving Bombay?'

'After one month.'

He felt the moon drain out of him. He had never given much thought to Chandni. Their meetings were brief and infrequent. He had assumed they would continue forever. Chandni was like the flower market—always there. How could she leave? He grit his teeth on the return ride, suddenly aware she was important in a way he could not define. But he was no stranger to loss. Hadn't he lost Kajol? Thankfully the tourist business was full of diversions. Soon Chandni would be part of his past and he would be soaring again.

Rahul liked strutting along the pier sporting his sunglasses. The rim touched his eyebrow, hugged his cheek, softening the glare. He would peer into mirrors of parked cars, satisfied that his reflection held a touch of mystery, authority. And one day a foreign face smiled back at him.

Andy and Steve were a different breed of tourist. Like Karen they broke boundaries, getting friendly with street kids, inviting them to their hotel. Andy was tall with floppy blonde hair and blue eyes. He took an instant fancy to Rahul.

'Ra-wool . . . what gorgeous eyes you have, Ra-wool . . . You like ice cream? I'll get some for you.'

Andy and Steve did not want to go sightseeing. Most of the time they hung around in their room with the boys, ordering endless rounds of ice cream, Cadbury's, Pepsi, biryani. Andy showed Rahul how to use the TV remote, let him play with his cell phone, showed him new video games. Playfully he sprayed Rahul with Denim on his earlobes, shoulders, armpits.

'Too young to shave but not for aftershave,' he joked as Rahul basked in pungent aromas. He had never been so pampered in his life.

'Here's something for you, gorgeous,' said Andy on a Wednesday Rahul would never forget. Rahul opened the cheap plastic bag and pulled out a pair of jeans and two shirts, his eyes shining. 'Like them? Go try them on,' urged Andy, pushing him towards the bathroom. In seconds Rahul was pulling off his shorts and shirt. 'Take a shower before wearing new clothes, Ra-wool.'

He fumbled, not knowing which the shower tap was. Andy was standing at the bathroom door. Stepping inside, he turned it on. Rahul gasped as water splashed over his head. Andy laughed. 'Never had a shower, Ra-wool? Let me soap your back.'

Rahul stood under hissing water as Andy's hands ran over him, back, front, buttocks, genitals. His breath became heavy, hands pressed down. He took off his clothes. 'Now rub me up, Ra-wool,' he murmured hoarsely, pressing the boy's hands over his genitals. 'Move faster . . . yes . . . yes!'

Afterwards he pressed Rahul to his stomach in a bear hug as water washed over them. Relaxing, Rahul wrapped his arms around Andy's buttocks. He had never felt so safe, so exhilarated. Through a slit in his eyes he watched a sliver of pink soap slide slowly towards the drain and get stuck on its raised ridge. He jabbed at the soap with his toe. Embrace broken, he wriggled free, impatient to try his new clothes. That evening Andy gave him a Walkman. He strutted off, earphones deafening him to street sounds.

It was Rahul who introduced Andy to charas, showing him how to roll a joint and light up. 'Wheee . . . beeeauooootiful,' enthused Andy as whirls wafted out of his nostrils. Rahul grinned. The Walkman was playing *Mousu-mousu hansi, deo ma lai-lai, mousu-mousu hansi deo*. Andy got up and took small steps to the lilting melody. 'Let's have something fast,' he said. Rahul rewound and fast-forwarded till he reached *Ek-do-teen* . . . Andy's eyes lit up. 'That's it, Ra-wool. Live it up!'

The month flew past in a heady cocktail of sex, grass and gifts the likes of which Rahul had never known. Clothes, perfumes, cassettes, chocolates. Andy had a box of 'toys'. A wig of short blue hair, another of long blonde hair. Silk stockings, lace panties, bras. Rahul would wear them and be photographed. Sometimes with nothing else on. Sometimes holding Andy's cock. Sometimes with Dinesh, also naked. Andy was obsessed with the camera.

For the last week the boys moved in with Andy and Steve, Rahul delighted to sleep on a bed again. The well-tipped hotel staff turned a blind eye to what went on behind closed doors. All too soon it was over. Andy and Steve returned to wherever they had come from. And the boys returned to the streets.

The first night on the Gateway's hard ledge was torture. The stone poked Rahul's bones, low tide released a foetid smell, mosquitoes buzzed menacingly. The milky glow around the moon was fringed by a rainbow ring, but the moon had shrunk to peanut size. Andy, Andy was all he could think about. 'I love you, gorgeous Ra-wool . . . I adore your gorgeous eyes . . . Next year I'll take you home. . .' The words kept ringing in his ears as the last whiffs of Denim lingered on his skin.

'They all say that. Forget him,' advised Dinesh. 'With your looks there'll be dozens of Andys for you.' But Rahul couldn't get this one out of his mind.

It was weeks since he had thought of Kajol; parting with Andy reopened the wound. He wondered whether her adoptive parents were kind like Andy, whether she was travelling in America, Italy, Germany. He knew the names of many countries. He had met their people. But Kajol, Chandni and Andy were lost.

Andy had left him a wad of five-hundred-rupee notes, plus a phone number and an email address. At last count Rahul's savings totalled six thousand and eight hundred rupees. This would take him closer to his dream-cab.

Igor from Sweden, Wilhelm from Amsterdam, Ronald from Perth. Gifting watches, Walkmans, cameras. Rahul sold them all, keeping Andy's Walkman even though it was older. He started charging a fee for sex—it was better than ending up with unwanted objects. He developed a base of 'regulars', local residents who paid two hundred rupees per hour. It was an easy life, getting pampered and earning at the same time. Better than the scramble for existence at railway stations.

Not all *firangs* wanted sex. Among the oddballs he befriended was Dieter, a German, who had come bicycling barefoot across two continents with his dog Lassie in a basket attached to the handlebar. His biggest kink was hugging, but nothing more. Rahul, Dinesh, Arvind had all been surprised by his bear hugs. 'Children need love more than money,' he declared as they hung around him expecting goodies to follow. There were none.

From each country he had crossed, Dieter had picked up a postal stamp of a monument, the easiest memento to carry. He spread them out like tiny colourful flags for the boys to admire. 'Travel expands experience,' he told them. 'When you travel you learn to do things by yourself, take risks, learn about different people, different cultures. You've travelled from your villages, I from my country. We have that in common.'

Rahul liked the comparison. But he couldn't fathom why Dieter wore no shoes. 'Road not hot on legs?' he asked.

'I haven't worn shoes for years. Except in snow. Of course streets in Europe are cleaner than in India.' He saw Rahul's puzzled expression and added, 'I like to feel the vibrations of Mother Earth, the pulse of traffic in the streets, the cushioning of lush grass. People lose sensation by wearing shoes.'

That made no sense. Rahul had been barefoot for years. He knew about pokes and cuts. Not vibrations—whatever they were.

'Tell me, do Indians sit cross-legged because it's an insult to show your soles to another?' asked Dieter.

That was a new one for Rahul. 'No, sir, it is insult to sit comfortable and put feet on Mother Earth,' he said with aplomb.

'Hmm. I never thought of that,' said the German thoughtfully. 'Why is this place named after a Greek god?' was the next question.

Having his impromptu reply accepted emboldened Rahul. He thought fast. 'Apollo ship sank on rocks near lighthouse. Brave captain saved sailors so Bunder named after ship.'

The German looked at him quizzically. The next day he picked up a guidebook that explained: Apollo Bunder got its name from palla fish, which were abundant in the waters before the pier was built in 1915. 'Nothing about your fake ship,' he said, amused.

He kept leafing through the book as the windows of the Taj reflected the rising sun, tinting its façade pink. Rahul played with Lassie, who had curled into a ball between them. 'Did you know Bombay was originally a fishing village?' Bombay, a village? Where on earth had Dieter picked up this book? 'Its seven islands have been connected. Look, here's a picture of where we are.'

Rahul grinned at a picture of the Gateway. 'So small it looks,' he giggled, sunglasses dangling from a loop in his jeans. 'Like your stamps.'

'The Gateway was built in 1924 to commemorate the visit of King George V and Queen Mary who were the first British monarchs to visit India,' continued Dieter, reading. He turned to Rahul playfully. 'You're a tourist guide but you know nothing!'

Dieter spent a week in Bombay, sleeping at the Gateway, letting Rahul ride his oversized bicycle. Late one night, as they shared a joint before stretching out to sleep on the ledge, Rahul asked, 'How you like India?'

Dieter was staring at a cluster of lights moving slowly through the dark sea. 'The Gateway is beautiful, you kids are great. But Bombay is too slick. Everyone is obsessed with money,' he said slowly. 'Look at all the American shops—McDonald's, Samsonite, Wrangler. Your people have made American money their god. India is no longer spiritual. It's an American market.'

Rahul thought Dieter was talking too fancy. He loved

the glitzy shops. It was okay for someone who didn't need money to criticize those who ran after it. But what about those who can only dream of goodies? Can they help being obsessed with money?

'On Tuesday I went to the Mombadevi temple from which Bombay gets its name,' continued the German. 'I offered a coconut, flowers, the priest gave me a sweet, someone put a garland around my neck. It was beautiful. I thought here's the real India in Bombay also. Then I went into the street with the usual mix of beggars, small shops, people pushing handcarts. Even in this very middle-class street almost every woman was wearing gold. Gold earrings, gold bangles, gold beads around the neck. At three o'clock in the afternoon! In my country where people are rich we only wear gold if we're going to the opera or for weddings. And in yours people wear gold all the time!'

He got up, dusting his pants as if to brush off the irony. 'I have to freshen up before turning in,' he said.

'Where are you going?' asked Rahul.

'To the Taj toilet,' replied Dieter.

'You go Taj to toilet . . .?'

'Ja.'

'They let you in?'

'Ja-ja. If you have white skin you can get away with many things in India.'

Without planning it, Rahul got into the Taj himself with Wanchai, a businessman from Bangkok. Wanchai came down in the early morning to feed pigeons from a large paper bag, a smile crinkling his thin lips as he scattered grain with wide sweeps of his hand. Rahul's Polaroid was loaded. Impulsively, he clicked photographs. As the chinky-eyed chap crumpled the empty bag, Rahul held them out.

'Good they are. How much?' inquired the smiling Thai.

'Four hundred.'

The man returned them to Rahul. 'Too much. You keep.'

'Two hundred,' bargained Rahul. 'Bombay souvenir. Wife will like, no?'

'No wife, no girl,' said the man. 'For one hundred, I take.'

Rahul agreed. The man slipped a hand into his pocket. 'Sorry. Money in hotel.' As Rahul's face fell he said, 'You come, I give you.'

Dark glasses shielded the excitement in his eyes. Even Dinesh had never been inside the Taj. He walked behind Wanchai to the gracious entrance where a tall turbaned usher stopped him. 'Boy not allowed, sir,' said the guard uncomfortably.

'He coming to my room. I have to give money, see?' said Wanchai, showing the guard the photographs. The man hesitated. 'I make you happy also, huh? *Chai-pani* . . .' Rahul smirked at his funny pronunciation.

Rahul could never have imagined such an elaborate stairway. Rising elegantly up the central foyer, its intricate wrought iron railings branched off into balconies along the wall, rising all the way up to the dome. He stood there gawking but Wanchai hustled him past a swinging door into an elevator where music was playing. Andy's music, but softer. They went up to the third floor, past the magnificent stairway, past paintings on walls, antique chests in the corridor and brass pots with drooping ferns till Wanchai took out a key and entered a room bathed in dappled light from slats between shutters. Rahul's eyes settled on the rumpled bed.

As Wanchai opened a drawer in the bedside table, Rahul said, 'I can give massage, sir. Very good massage.'

Wanchai drew back. 'Massage?' he asked, eyes narrowing.

Rahul grinned, wondering how much he could charge. 'Body massage,' he said, running his tongue over his lips.

'I see. One muscle massage. One muscle grows bigger, gets more massage, right?'

His grin grew wider. The man had caught on. A thousand, he decided. Anyone staying here would surely pay. Rahul was confident about plying his trade. He might even be put on to other clients . . .

'In my country we arrest boys for soliciting off the street,' said Wanchai severely.

'I can make happy, sir,' said Rahul.

'How old are you? Twelve? Thirteen? Haven't you heard of AIDS?'

'No problem, sir. I got condom.'

'Get out before I have you thrown out!' roared the Thai in a voice that pierced through Rahul's dream cloud.

His grin faded. 'But-but sir . . . money . . .?'

Wanchai's face turned red. Grabbing the photographs, he tore them into fragments and flung them at Rahul. 'Get out of my room before I have you arrested!' he shouted again, reaching for the telephone.

Rahul ran out. He ran all the way down the never-ending stairway without turning back. For those few minutes he was scared, but back on the seafront he felt triumphant. He was one up on Dinesh. He had entered the Taj.

Sadak Chhaap

Rahul and Dinesh were sharing their first joint of the day with the Walkman playing *It's a rich man's world* when Shankar arrived at the adda, looking excited. The tea was still hot though the stove was off. Two loaves of pao remained warm on the *dekchi*'s lid.

'You boys must be thirteen-fourteen, right? Know any girls your age? Living alone like you?' asked Shankar as he poured himself tea in Rahul's glass.

They looked at each other and shrugged. Chandni was married and away. The few others they knew lived with their families, and they didn't know them well.

'Why?' asked Dinesh.

'An Arab is looking for a wife. He's ready to pay twenty thousand. If the girl is beautiful he'll go up further.'

'Take him to a film star!'

Shankar looked at Rahul scornfully. 'You think stars go for peanuts?' Going down on his haunches he took out a cigarette from his shirt pocket, tapping its end to empty tobacco on a small piece of paper. Mixing it with a pinch of charas he began refilling the cigarette roll.

'I thought you didn't smoke.'

'Once in a while,' he said, lighting up. 'I'm serious about this, boys. Think of all the pretty girls you know.'

'Kajol.'

'Madhuri.'

'Aishwarya, Rekha, Simi . . .'

'Sushmita, Rani, Tabu, Preity . . .'

'Stop joking, yaar! A lot of money is at stake!'

'Who's going to pay twenty thousand rupees for a street girl? You're talking five-star money!'

'He's not paying for one night. He wants to marry her. He'll go up to one lakh dowry for giving her a new life.'

Shankar became quiet as charas loosened the knots in his chest. Lowering himself to the floor, he stretched his legs, tipping over the tea as he reached for another drag. Dinesh mopped up, pouring the last dregs from the *dekchi* into a glass and handing it to Shankar.

'Where did you pick this one up? The airport again?' asked Rahul.

'Nah. He had my contact from an Arab I helped last year.'

'Helped find a woman or a wife?'

'Same thing.' He jerked his head back as hot tea scalded his tongue. Putting down the glass he pulled out a checked handkerchief from his pocket, wrapped it around the glass and slurped.

'*Sala badmash,*' sneered Dinesh. 'Are you a *lakhopati* yet?'

'If I weren't a *lakhopati* would I own my cab?'

'What commission should we charge for helping Shri Lakhopati become Shri Crorepati?'

'Stop fooling, boys. I'll come back when you're sober. Stay away from charas for a few hours so we can talk.' Returning to the cab he switched on the ignition, billowing black exhaust into the adda. 'Remember, girls below fifteen,' he called. Then he was off.

'Is he serious?' asked Rahul, staring after the diminishing cab.

Dinesh stubbed out the joint against the pavement. 'With Shankar you can never tell. He's got his finger in many pies.'

'How does he operate?' wondered Rahul.

'Ask him to take you along.'

Since none of his contacts could rustle up a girl Shankar

had to go to a dalal. All the way he kept grumbling to Rahul about the heavy brokerage dalals charge, how Rahul should befriend girls, take a commission, make business more lucrative for them both. Rahul listened with a growing sense of unease.

Gauri-behn turned out to be a woman of fifty, fair, with thinning hair tied into a tight knot behind her head. A black mole to the right of her lips had a single black hair growing out. She was as shrewd as Shankar.

'How old is your client?' was her first question.

'Forty-five, fifty.'

'With grey hair?'

'A little.'

'Which means he's at least sixty-five.' She paused to let it sink in that she knew the trade better than Shankar. 'You want a fifteen-year-old girl for a sixty-five-year-old man?'

Rahul gasped.

'He's not so old, Gauri-behn . . .'

'The last client you brought could barely walk.'

'But he paid for the girl.'

'God knows what mincemeat he made of her.'

'You always get your money from me, Gauri-behn. We're professionals.'

Her eyes narrowed. 'I'm not interested in twenty-thirty-thousand deals.'

'Did I offer you such an insulting fee? You'll get nothing less than fifty.'

'The girl's family will also demand.'

'These are not the old days, Gauri-behn. We could lose him to Hyderabad.'

'Sixty is my last price.'

'I must also get something.'

She ignored him. 'Fifty per cent before the viewing. The balance before the girl crosses my threshold. I can show three girls.'

'Below fifteen?'

She stood up, towering over them disdainfully. 'Don't I always deliver?' she said, leading them to the exit where she paused, twirling the hair on her mole. 'I have a twelve-year-old virgin,' she said as a deliberate afterthought. 'But her price is not negotiable.'

Shankar's eyes lit up. He walked back to the chair and sat down. 'My client might be interested. What's her price?'

'Two lakhs. Not one rupee less.'

'Is she . . . is she pretty? Developed?' he asked, gesturing curves.

'She will grow.'

A bit more bargaining and the deal was sealed at one-lakh-fifty. Rahul left the marriage broker's flat in a daze. 'This is . . . selling girls . . . to old men,' he gasped in disbelief. 'Why so much for the small girl?'

'Don't you know? The first man to deflower a virgin is cured of disease.'

He felt the bile rising from the pit of his stomach. 'That old Arab has disease?'

Shankar shrugged. 'Who knows?'

It was revolting. Rahul felt an intense need to get away from Shankar. He didn't want to see the girl who was being sent to her doom. He didn't want to see the Arab against whom he was helpless. He hated Shankar; his money was blacker than his cab. As they stopped at a traffic light Rahul jumped out, leaving the door swinging jerkily.

His body was shaking with disgust. He walked with long rhythmic strides, wanting to get away from the odious deal he had witnessed. Suddenly he thought of Chandni. What had become of her? Had she been married off to some old Arab? She, with her delicate designs made from flowers. *Veni*s for other women, rarely herself. She was part of his past. A long receded, innocent past, and still precious.

The thought of her abandoned to an Arab was excruciating. He had no idea where she was, whether she needed a friend, how he could help even if he found her. All he could do was hope her mother was real, that she had found Chandni a genuine partner, that his friend would not be miserable for life. But he would never know the truth.

Sheer animal magnetism attracted Rahul to Greg, who sat shirtless at the Gateway's pier in jeans and a sleeveless jacket, blowing smoke rings at the sea. A small gold stud flashed in his left ear. Each finger had a ring with a different stone.

Rahul approached him with his hello-new-to-Bombay line. Greg ignored him, continuing his abstracted stance, exhaling between gold-edged teeth. Rahul smelt the smoke, smiled and moved away. But he kept observing the tall, well-built man, hair in a straggly ponytail. He stayed in the same position, only the hand moving to his mouth and back, flicking off ash. After a while he lay on the ledge and seemed to fall asleep.

Rahul hovered around, attracted by an energy he could not explain. Almost an hour passed before the man got up, seeming to register his surroundings for the first time. 'Hello, new to Bombay?' began Rahul again, sidling up.

'Hi. The name's Greg. What's yours?'

'Rahul.'

Greg looked him up and down, making no secret of liking what he saw. Rahul felt a tingling down his spine. 'Join me for a beer?' asked Greg.

Rahul shook his head. 'No drink. You got cigarette?'

Greg laughed. 'Sure do,' he said, tossing Rahul a pack.

Rahul lit up, disappointed—they were regular cigarettes. 'You want hotel?' he asked.

Greg looked amused. 'No chum, I'm staying with a friend. Here he comes.'

Rahul turned to face a bald, middle-aged Indian incongruously wearing a wide-brimmed straw hat.

'Narain, meet Rahul,' said Greg, dragging the tongue on his palate to stretch out the 'l'. 'I invited Rahul to join us for beer but he doesn't drink.'

'You can have Pepsi,' smiled Narain, flashing white teeth.

In the restaurant they ignored him, speaking in a language he didn't understand. Five beers and three Pepsis later they were ready to leave.

'Bye Rahul, see ya t'morrow,' slurred Greg, tousling his hair. The touch was electric.

Rahul took Dinesh to the Gateway the next morning after bathing in the public loo, wet hair flattened against his scalp. Sticking his tongue between lips he ran a narrow comb through curly hair and stepped away from the mirror to preen. With a stylish swish of the arm he perched sunglasses on his nose, blinking at the sudden change of light. When he stepped out, Dinesh let out a low whistle.

Greg appeared at around two o'clock. The sight of him set off alarm bells in Dinesh's head. 'Be careful. This guy's not regular,' cautioned Dinesh as he backed away. 'I'm leaving.'

The meetings continued for a week. Always the same. Greg, lost to the world of smoke, meeting Rahul, Narain appearing, hat flopped over egghead, beer at Baghdadi's, then back to Narain's. The only change was in the parting.

From a friendly tousle to a hug, to suggestive touches. A building up of momentum. Rahul trembled in excitement, knowing what was coming, not knowing when.

A few days, and Greg abruptly said, 'How much for spending the night with us?'

'Both?' asked Rahul, wondering if Dinesh had been right after all. Greg nodded. 'Normal rate, five hundred for one hour.'

'For the whole night, Rahul. Come on. Think fast.'

'Ten thousand,' he blurted.

'Done. Tomorrow's the night. We meet at eight.'

Another Andy, exulted Rahul. Ten thousand rupees would swell his savings. The dream cab was there for his taking. They wanted to do it together, they were willing to pay for it. Maybe he would learn some new tricks. He splurged on Denim cologne in anticipation.

The whole week Greg had been in the same clothes, but when he came to pick up Rahul he was wearing a shirt. Greg gave directions to the cab. He seemed to know Bombay well. They sped away from familiar Colaba, past Cuffe Parade with its high-rise apartment blocks into unfamiliar territory with sentry points at street corners. The cab stopped at a bungalow bordered by a chain fence, but before Rahul could take in the surroundings he was whisked indoors. A hatless Narain opened the door before they pressed the bell, bald pate gleaming. He led them to an air-conditioned bedroom with a huge circular bed. A shapeless beanbag sat in a corner. Posters of Sylvester Stallone and Bruce Lee adorned the walls. Everything was red—curtains, carpet, bedcover, furniture. Only the ceiling was white with a tiny red fan over the bed.

'Like our Moulin Rouge?' asked Greg, dropping his

shirt on the floor. His sunburnt torso was etched with an outline of the sleeveless jacket. Seeing Rahul's consternation Greg laughed. 'Get outta your clothes. Wanna use the bathroom?'

Red dominated the bathroom as well. Red toilet bowl, red wash basin, red tiles, red towels. And on the shelf under the mirror, a brown porcelain scorpion. The wall held an assortment of leather belts and chains but no hook for clothes. A life-sized male nude stared at Rahul from behind the door.

He undressed, peed, slung his clothes over his shoulder and opened the door. A naked Greg jumped up, pointing the steel blade of a knife at Rahul's phallus. Rahul screamed. Narain clicked fast, capturing his terrified expression.

Instinctively Rahul covered his crotch with his clothes. Greg's knife flicked them away. 'Relax, Rahul, we won't hurt you,' he purred. 'You're being paid to do a job.'

Wide-eyed, Rahul gaped from Greg to Narain and back. Their teeth flashed ominous smiles. A shiver ran down his back softly like a spider as realization dawned that he was in for a bigger adventure than he had expected.

'Pl-please . . . let me go,' he croaked, as the impulse to escape hammered inside his head.

'Too late, Rahul. You made a commitment. We've got the whole night. You'll go when we're finished.'

He dropped his threatening stance. 'C'mon, man. Enjoy yourself. We're just having fun.' He put an arm around Rahul's waist and lowered his face, giving Rahul a full-blooded kiss on the mouth. His teeth felt like scorpions, his body smelt of sweat. Rahul could not extricate himself from the vice-like grip on his mouth. He shuddered. Never had the impulse to run been so strong. But he was naked. His clothes had been taken away.

'Please let me go,' he pleaded again, on the verge of tears.

'Want a joint?' asked Greg laconically, ignoring him. Rahul nodded.

Narain was loading fresh film into the camera. Greg sprawled diagonally across the bed. Rahul slunk into the beanbag. 'Come to me, Rahul,' slurred Greg, dragging the last syllable as he had done the first time they met. Rahul cowered deeper into the beanbag, clutching the joint. 'I said, come to me,' repeated Greg, his voice turning sharp. Rahul stayed put. Greg got up and yanked Rahul by the hand, forcing his mouth on the boy's again. Narain was ready with the camera, zeroing in on Rahul's fingers as they closed over an erect penis.

The games went on all night. Different postures, different objects. One photograph had Rahul's mouth gagged by a chain. For another he was strung by a leather belt from the fan with Greg ejaculating under him. It was the longest night of his life. Tasting fear in the most intense form he had known, he screamed, cried, pleaded, but the more he begged to be released the more Greg got turned on. When at last his clothes were returned, he staggered away, half deranged. Instead of the promised ten he was paid only two thousand.

Milk bottles stood outside Narain's door as Rahul stumbled out, too dazed to register relief. He walked blindly, not caring where he was going, just wanting to get away. He knew they were not far from the Gateway. Greg's cab had taken barely twenty minutes. But the area had no familiar landmarks. Nor was there a paan-wallah, a shop or street-dweller to ask directions. He tottered like a drunk, veering from lamp post to wall. In desperation he searched for a cab, any means to get away. To where? He did not want to go back to the Gateway. Nor could he face Karim-bhai at the barsati. And Sharan was out of the question.

Aimlessly he staggered around till his feet could no longer carry him. Then he hailed a cab. For want of any other place he said Radio Club, his eyes blank. When he got off the seat, his pants were stained with blood.

Whoa, we're going to Ibiza, the island . . . Whoa, we're gonna have a party . . . in the Mediterranean Sea. Andy's music seeped into him, blanking out the present. Andy's Walkman was glued to his ear. Andy's voice on the telephone. 'Don't cry, Ra-wool. Tell me what happened . . . Do you need money, Ra-wool? I love you, gorgeous . . . I'm coming next year . . . We'll go to Goa . . .'

An intense need to blank out, forget. But images die hard. His head rolled, fingers clutching hair clumps, pulling till his scalp prickled, driving sleep away. Gritting teeth, clenching eyes, squeezing vision out, jaw contorting mouth into hideous grimaces. Food rattling. Stomach-souring hiccups. Locked jaws sealing bile. Threatening vomit. Or shit.

He ended up asking Andy for the thing he needed least— money. His need was for comfort, support, nurturing. But Andy was too far away.

In a week he switched from charas to garda; his regular supplier, in a rare fit of generosity, offered free trips to tide over his depression. Brown sugar deadened more effectively. A grateful Rahul inhaled bitter fumes, one nostril at a time, from powder burnt on silver foil, horror images replaced by the red of a cosy womb, the red of a floating dupatta, red against blue sky, translucent, transparent blue. In moments of clarity he imagined Andy dancing at the promised beach party in faraway Goa, far away next year. And Kajol? Was she also in the Mediterranean, like Andy? Or in Manchester near Karen? What if she were in New York, where Greg lived?

He became scared of accosting tourists. Suppose they turned out to be like Greg? How was he to tell? He dare not risk another mistake.

Ribbons of blue, remind me of you; ribbons of red, of the day that my heart bled . . .

The sea changed from blue to sunset-scarlet. A hand emerged from crashing waves. Holding a red hibiscus. Wriggling, flailing, dropping the flower in a sea of black blood. Black swallowing red. Floating red. Crabs shooting out from a bloody sea, crawling on water. Like Christ, the magician.

Dead music. Dead Walkman. The choice between batteries and fix was no choice. Money reached a dangerous low.

'Try direct,' suggested the seller of garda. 'Stronger result.'

Without garda—and with it, too—Greg and Narain haunted. The knife tip, twisted chains, twisted postures, twisted minds. Porcelain scorpion coming alive. Chasing. Greg chasing, Narain going click-click-click.

Trips too short. Becoming shorter. Sun, moon, sea, sky, receding as rocks hammered inside his head. Intestines twisted into painful knots, releasing rivers of sweat down a shivering body. Oblivion blotting out horrorscapes. A voice, resembling his, cursed the sun for freezing. Rahul barely recognized it. Waking with bodyache and vague hunger. Throat refusing to swallow. Bowels letting go. A huge effort to stagger out of the adda for the next round of chasing.

Sadak Chhaap

Rahul succumbed to the vendor. Bought a vial. Then he met Harsh who showed him how to boil and dissolve powder in lime water, cool and strain it, fill a hypodermic needle. Finding the vein was painful. Harsh tied a rubber tightly around Rahul's upper arm. As a vein bulged, he jabbed thrice before making the connection. Rahul winced as he drew blood in and out of the syringe to mix it with heroin. Then he shot into Rahul's vein.

Dopey minutes. Then he was swooping and soaring as colours swirled, mushroomed and exploded around him. Unknown, unimagined forms. Worlds beyond the world. Sky beyond the stars. Stars emanating new stars. *Dum maro dum . . . mit jaye gam . . . bolo subah shaam . . . Hare Krishna Hare Ram . . .* Rahul was one with the blue god, merging into space, raining stolen buttermilk on indifferent trees.

Oh I need your lovin' eight days of the week . . . Notes bouncing bubbles. Exploding into rainbows. Fragrant denim rainbows. Songs amplified without Walkman. Turning heavy, falling. Tree stumps hurtling through a birdless sky. Missing earth. Crashing. Black, eternal abyss. His legs thrashed empty air. The world was upside down. Muscles contracted, rolling his body into a ball, toes clenched tight like fists. Howls ending in a whine. He broke into a cold sweat, shivering.

Dinesh was peering into his face. 'You're on a bad trip,' he said, as Rahul struggled to sit, his syringe a ridge among scattered stubs. Wincing, he slipped down again.

'I . . . I'm okay,' he mumbled, resting his head against the wall. It was too heavy for his neck. He had eaten nothing for two days but wasn't hungry.

Dinesh examined him. 'You were shouting for someone

called Kajol,' he said, perplexed. 'Who's Kajol?'

Rahul didn't answer. Dinesh tried again. 'Who's Kajol?' He remained blank. 'Must be some old flame,' muttered Dinesh, giving up.

Rahul pounced on him like a tiger. 'She's my daughter!' he screamed.

Dinesh backed off. 'Oh boy, you've got it real bad,' he mumbled, moving away.

Hand splotched with needle jabs. Impossible to find a vein. Tremors made fingers leaves in the wind. Hand abandoned, Rahul searched his leg for hidden veins. He licked the needle, made contact at the ankle, and closed his eyes dopily. Till next time. . .

The garda seller's mood changed. Prices doubled and rose again. Begging left him cold. In desperation Rahul accosted tourists, need overpowering fear. A putrid smell emanated from his body. Giving him money was the only way to get rid of him.

Body heavy, head heavier. And painful bones. Rahul had not known he had so many bones. Did he once live in a body without being conscious of its bones? Anchor-heavy bones. Impossible to move his bones, impossible to move without them. But imperative to move, imperative to reach garda. A drag from Dinesh helps. Only for a few minutes.

Clutching the dead Walkman Rahul clawed the wall and staggered out of the adda, his hair a matted mess. The better pair of jeans had already been sold. Also Andy's shoes. The Walkman's turn had come.

At the sight of a yellow-and-black cab, he stopped in his tracks. What happened to his dream? His eyes turned liquid, melting out of their sockets. He slumped to the floor and leaned against the wall. But there was no wall. He fell flat on the road, body heavier than a house. Karen's glasses crushed by a flailing elbow. The wheels of a parked truck became a wall. No Dinesh to beg a drag from. Rahul picked up the Walkman tenderly and put it under his shirt. He struggled up, avoiding shards. The rose-tinted glasses had shattered. He had to leave them behind.

'No! No, *bachcha*! I will not give you money! Look at your condition!' Karim-bhai's voice was shaking.

'It's my money. I want it,' snarled Rahul.

'Of course it's your money. But I won't help you ruin yourself. Where have you been all these months?'

'Same place,' mumbled Rahul. 'I want. . .'

'Gateway of India? Tourist business? Take me for a fool!' blazed Karim-bhai, looking aghast at the dishevelled, sunken-eyed teenager he barely recognized. Still in shock, he called to a boy standing nearby. 'Run the stall. I'm going out,' he said, leading Rahul away.

The waiter clunked two glasses of water on their table in a dingy restaurant. Karim-bhai took a gulp. 'Two kheema-paos and black coffee,' ordered Karim-bhai, remembering Rahul's penchant for kheema.

Rahul sat, head hunched into shoulders, barely touching the kheema. Though he hadn't eaten in days the sight of food nauseated him. Karim-bhai dipped a piece of bread into the gravy and held it to Rahul's lips. Rahul pushed it away.

'How long have you been like this?' asked Karim-bhai.

'Mind your own business. Give me my money.'

'When you are well.'

'Give me my money now,' shouted Rahul. People turned

to stare. Karim-bhai asked for the bill. As the waiter put it on their table Rahul lunged for Karim-bhai's wallet and tried to run. He crashed into the next table. The waiter pinned him down.

'Thief! Thief! This man is a thief!' yelled Rahul, grabbing a knife and staggering towards Karim-bhai. Karim-bhai did not move. Four men restrained Rahul. Bloodshot eyes glared, animal-like. In a sudden fit he flung off the hands, flung away the knife, grabbed a fifty-rupee note from the cash counter and ran.

The moon bit off a clump of cloud. Swallowed it into its sickle of a belly. The cloud gobbled up the moon. Blinding stars. Scorpions chased black holes. Bottomless pits with slippery walls. The painful waking hour. Emptiness layered on emptiness. Blood, bones liquefying. Black, stagnant. Torpedoes from the earth's centre crashing into the moon, smashing it, raining slivers of milky moon-drops. Sticky, milky mock-drops.

Screaming, Rahul woke up in a cold sweat. In an unknown place, alone. In lucid moments he blamed Karim-bhai for his state. If the fruit vendor hadn't stolen his money he wouldn't be reduced to begging, to facing insults. Karim-bhai would have to be taught a lesson. He would be thrashed till he returned Rahul's money. It was a breach of trust. For the rest of his life he would regret double-crossing Rahul. Rahul would teach him a lesson, a lesson he would never forget.

Where was he? Who were all these people? These whirring sounds? And clattering? Why did he see two of everything? Were they real or imaginary?

Clouds thinned into soft focus. The station was real. Straight lines with tracks curving away. Which station? An engine's spotlight pierced the dark. He saw the stone steps of an overbridge. The only way out. A wisp of memory. He was on his way to Karim-bhai's. To kill him. He had no weapon, no plan of action. Only strong desire. He had to climb the overbridge to reach the road. Which road? He could only find out once he was out. He lurched towards the railing. Before he could steady himself, a khaki-uniformed man jabbed a lathi into his ribs.

'Eh, charasi. Follow me.' The order was barked in a voice that had to be obeyed.

Rahul could barely keep up with the man's stride. He briskly walked the full length of the platform, all the way to the dark end where three others were waiting. Two junkies like himself, and an official with a torch. A canvas stretcher lay on the floor. The junkies picked it up and moved to the tracks. The officers followed, Rahul stumbling behind.

'A man has fallen off the train,' said the officer who had ordered Rahul to follow. 'We have to find him in the dark.'

Mechanically, Rahul did what he was told. Walking with people felt better than walking alone. The officer flashing the torch was far ahead. Rahul staggered behind like a ghostly shadow. Then he tripped and toppled to his knees. His palm sank into ooze, black and viscous. He floundered, lifting it up. Something slimy slithered towards him. 'Ah! Aaah! Aaaaah!'

'What's the matter with him?' asked the officer, turning the torch.

'Aah! Eeh! Aah!' screamed Rahul uncontrollably.

A finger had got hooked into his shirt. A grotesque, disembodied hand dangled from Rahul's elbow, dripping blood.

'Put it on the stretcher!' commanded the officer.

Rahul could not move. He was shaking from head to foot, the hand swaying hideously from his sleeve. One of the junkies disengaged the hand.

'Now look for the body,' said the officer, looking at Rahul pityingly. 'We should have caught an older boy.'

'They're all the same,' replied his colleague. 'For twenty rupees they'll do anything.'

Rahul waited for his twenty rupees. He had earned it the hard way.

Like a mad dog he returned to drown in his vomit. Squatting with the junkies on his raw rectum, shaky fingers searching for veins. Each clutching precious notes. A note fluttered to the floor. Rahul lunged, grabbed. It escaped into other hands.

'Mine!'

'No mine!'

'I said mine!'

'It's not! It's mine!'

The flash of a blade. Wild slashes. Rahul screamed. He raised a hand to the stinging cut on his cheek. The same hand. Red, wet, slimy, slippery. 'Aaaaah!'

Then colour died. A single crow dropped like a bundle into a sea of putrescence. Dead birds on pulp that had once been moss. Slimy fields lapping liquefied forests. Hand plunging. Recoiling from glutinous soil. Black grass. Dung-coloured flowers. Spiders weaving a sword-edged carpet. Acid leaves stuck to the body. Twitching movements of a madman not even the terror of an unhinging mind could control. Imperative to be free of stinging leaves. Of a clutching hand emerging from cracks in concrete wall. Dead fingers swarming like monster mosquitoes.

Trembling fingers lifted the handset of a public phone. Through a fog Rahul guessed at a number. 'Childline . . .?' he asked in a hoarse, broken voice.

'This is Childline.'

'I . . . I need help.'

'Where are you?'

'Station.'

'Which station?'

'I . . . I don't know. Is . . . is Victor there?'

'Who's that?'

'Is Shekhar there?'

'I am Shekhar.'

'She-khar . . .' he broke into sobs. 'Shekhar . . . this is Rahul.'

'Rahul! Where are you, Rahul? We've been thinking about you for months!'

Rahul started sobbing. Shekhar held on. When Rahul was able to control himself, he said, 'Give the phone to someone who can tell us where you are.'

Rahul handed the phone to an irate shopkeeper and passed out.

eighteen

Victor reached first. He found Rahul slumped against the phone booth. A skeleton with long matted hair, shrivelled skin sinking into hollows between ribs.

'Eh, Rahul. What are you doing here?' he called, patting his cheeks.

Rahul stirred. 'Help . . .' he slurred. 'I need . . .'

'Come on. Get up. I've come to help you.'

His eyes opened to a blurred silhouette, then focussed slowly. His lips parted in a smile. 'Vi-cky . . .' he said, and slumped again.

'C'mon Rahul. You're coming home with me,' said Victor briskly, slipping an arm under Rahul's shoulder and propping him up. His head rolled down to Victor's shoulder. 'I can't carry you . . . You're too heavy. Try to move a bit.'

'Pain. Whole body is paining . . .'

'We're going to get you well.'

'Well . . .?' said Rahul with the crooked smile of a child who half understands. 'I'm okay . . . Just need little . . .'

'Food, bath, bandage.'

'Bandage? For what?'

'Your cheek.'

Rahul raised his hand to the blood-encrusted scab.

Memory returned in a titanic wave. He shuddered, broke into a cold sweat, shivering. 'Vicky . . . don't leave me Vicky . . .' he whispered, clinging to Victor.

Victor ruffled his matted hair. 'I'm taking you home. It's not far.'

'We're near Sharan . . .?'

'Near our house.'

'House?'

'We are too old for Sharan,' said Victor with a smile as Rahul staggered up. 'Smaller boys need space. Shekhar, Anand and I share a *kholi* at Sion Koliwada.'

They hobbled out of the station into teeming traffic, Rahul leaning heavily on Victor. Every hundred yards he would slump, threatening to topple, but Victor held on, propping him against a car or wall. When they reached the shack Shekhar was stirring khichdi over a kerosene stove.

'When did you last have a meal?' Rahul couldn't remember. 'Suck a lime,' said Shekhar, handing him a sliced nimbu. Rahul put it to his lips and withdrew, making a face. 'I know you need a painkiller. But not on an empty stomach.'

Shekhar held a spoonful of khichdi to Rahul's lips. Rahul took it into his dry mouth. It stuck to his tongue, palate, inner cheeks. He tried to swallow. It became a lump in his throat. He spat it out. Shekhar gave him a sip of water. 'Try again,' he said, spooning out more khichdi. Rahul managed to down a small bit.

Khichdi in his belly helped him register his surroundings. They were in a small shed in a colony of shanties. Tin walls and roof. Three trunks piled in a corner. Another pile of bedrolls. Two folding chairs and the bench on which he was sitting. Clothes on a plastic line running across the shed. And a calendar with Lakshmi serene on a lotus.

'Is this your own place?' he asked in wonder.

They nodded. 'Sharan gave us a loan to buy it. We've started paying back.'

'How?'

'I'm on the staff of Childline. Pukka salary. And Victor . . .'

'I've opened a pao-bhaji stall with Anand. Also with a loan. And I go to night school. First year commerce.'

There was pride on his friends' faces. But the ache was returning to his bones. Clutching his ribs he groaned, 'Pain . . . too much . . . too much pain . . .'

Shekhar slipped a tablet onto Rahul's palm. Trembling fingers placed it at the back of his tongue. Rahul took a swig of water. But the tablet stuck. He took another swig. It stayed lodged in his throat. He spat it out, close to tears. 'I can't swallow,' he said.

Shekhar took another tablet, crushed it to powder between two spoons, dissolved it in water. 'Sip this,' he told Rahul, handing him the glass. He downed it in a single gulp.

He shut his eyes, resting his head against the tin wall. It felt good to be among friends. It was ages since he had felt secure. A long time since anyone had done anything for him. 'Where's Bablu?' he asked.

'At Sharan. He's become food minister.'

Rahul smiled. Remembering it was Bablu who proposed him as health minister, he asked, 'Are hospitals as bad as I remember?'

The boys laughed.

'Come, let me look at your cheek.'

Rahul turned his face to Shekhar, who had taken a box out of a trunk. He winced as Shekhar dipped a wad of cotton in Dettol-spiked water and began wiping the wound. The pain was nothing compared to the pain in his bones. Shekhar put gauze and two strips of plaster across Rahul's cheek. 'The wound is deep on one side. We'll watch it a couple of days. If it doesn't get better I'll take you to hospital.'

'You're not health minister now . . .' groaned Rahul.

'Oh yes, he is,' Victor piped in. 'The rules in this house are made by the prime minister and health minister. Visitor-citizens have to obey.'

Rahul laughed, puckering cheek muscles making him wince. It was good to feel safe. He lay back on the bench and stared at the corrugated ceiling. His eyes drooped shut. He fell asleep. No dreams. No nightmares. Hours later he woke to the sound of sizzling oil and pungent aromas. Eyelids fluttered open to darkness broken by the off-and-on glow of a neon light. No one was in the shed, but sounds and smells wafted in from the door. He could hear onions being chopped, masalas being ground. Victor and a less familiar voice spoke in low voices. His bones hurt less now. He lifted an arm to test them, sat up slowly, gingerly stepped on his feet. His neck could carry his head.

'*Kya baat hai*! You look like a ghost!' exclaimed Anand, sizing him up.

'If I'd died I'd have become a ghost,' said Rahul matter-of-factly.

Victor looked up sharply. 'No talk of dying. You haven't spent fourteen years on earth to quit so soon.'

'We *sadak chhaap*-wallahs are dispensable. Like *kuchra*.'

'*Chup*!'

'It's true, isn't it? Who cares about us?'

The moon was full, its silvery light etching the dark slum into soft silhouettes. The boys ignored it, huddling into a companionable knot around the hissing stove, oily dark complexions glowing in the incandescence of the lunar dish.

Victor began speaking slowly. 'We knew a boy called Rahul who became a father at the age of ten. Do you remember him?' Rahul's lip quivered.

'Our friend Rahul was going to make something of his life. He was determined not to remain *sadak chhaap*. He told us about Govinda rising from a banana seller to stardom. He told us about Vinod driving a Maruti. He told us he was going to be like them, get off the streets, succeed.'

Victor paused, watching his words sink in. A tear struggled with lashes. As legs wobbled, Rahul searched for something to sit on but both chairs were occupied. He lowered himself to the ground, wincing as he placed all his body weight first on his left buttock, then on the right. Then he squatted, facing the fat, round moon.

'Then our friend Rahul disappeared,' continued Victor. 'We didn't hear from him for months. He forgot us. Only kept in touch with his best friend Bablu who told us he was making lots of money. Giving gifts, treats. We were happy for Rahul. And we told each other, if Rahul can do it, so can we.'

Rahul gave up. Tears escaped down sunken cheeks and dripped off his chin. Victor's voice was reaching into starved areas of his psyche. Parched dry.

'Suddenly Rahul vanished completely,' came Victor's

voice. 'Someone said he'd gone to America. We couldn't dream of going to America. But the thought of Rahul in America propelled us. We had to make something of ourselves in Bombay.'

Rahul put his palms over his ears to block the voice he wanted so much to hear. If only it had come at another time, before things went wrong. To escape the persistent voice he looked at the sky. A cloud lined with colours of a rainbow dimmed the moonlight. Before his eyes it morphed from a sheep into a rabbit, the moon peeping out from an eye.

'Out of the blue we got a phone call,' continued Victor. 'Our friend Rahul was lost. He was desperate. He needed us. And we rushed to him. He has been our role model. How can we let him die?'

His sobs came in short gasps. Victor made no effort to stop them, waiting for the storm to abate. Much later, Anand handed Rahul a plate. But the spicy rice and chicken gagged his throat. His body had become used to being without food. It rebelled against being overloaded. Especially when it couldn't get what it wanted—a fix. Somehow he managed to swallow some biryani. Somehow he managed to avoid salting it with his tears. Somehow he found the will to hold it down. And asked, 'Where's Shekhar?'

'He's bringing Aparna-didi to see you.'

He was still wearing the filthy clothes Victor had picked him up in. He looked at himself self-consciously. 'I . . . I can't meet didi like this.'

'There's a tap at the end of this row of sheds. Go, wash yourself. I've taken out a shirt and shorts for you.'

Pain was returning. Stomach churning. Need growing. The shirt, shorts and a towel were lying on top of a trunk.

He picked them up, eyes roving, searching for something small. He spotted a watch, slipped it into the pocket of the shorts and walked out. Bones turning to lead again. Stomach heaving rebellion. Wanting to expel, eject. With much effort Rahul lumbered towards the tap, holding his stomach in—unsuccessfully. Clutching a lamp post he vomited. Coughing. Sputtering.

Victor ran up, supporting his convulsing body. He took the clothes from his hand, threw them across his shoulder, jumping as the watch fell out. His eyes flashed accusingly but he controlled himself, picked it up and strapped it on his wrist.

Rahul's face fell. 'How did you drop your watch?' he stuttered.

'It fell out of the clothes.'

'H-how did it get there?'

'You know as well as I do.'

He was crestfallen. But pain was hammering his blood. Demanding relief. 'Give me . . . some. . .' he pleaded, clutching Victor's elbow.

Victor disengaged himself. He put an arm around Rahul and led him firmly to the tap. Water was gushing into a gleaming brass *handi*. Despite the late hour, a woman waited beside it. The sight had Rahul in tears. Inexplicably he sat on the stone used for beating clothes, weeping copiously.

The woman looked at him pityingly. 'Is he sick?' she asked Victor.

'You could say that.'

She picked up the vessel, straddled it across her hip. He wept louder. She turned back, face suffused with compassion. A child ran up and tugged at her sari. She followed the child into a tin shed.

Victor splashed water on Rahul's face. The crying subsided. Rahul squatted under the tap, shivering, making no effort to reach for the soap, no attempt to scrub. Victor took the soap, rubbed it into Rahul's matted hair. As lice appeared on the foam, he pulled away. Heedless of howled protests, he dunked the head under the tap, lice raining onto the washing stone. Then he ran soap over Rahul's back, chest, legs. At last Rahul stood up, dripping water from the *langot* around his loins. Victor threw him the towel and stood away as Rahul rubbed himself dry.

The pain was excruciating, the need overpowering, the wait interminable.

Rahul sat with eyes closed, moaning, head rolling, hands restless, clutching and releasing his shirt, scratching his scalp, rubbing the scar on his cheek. 'She's not coming!' he yelled suddenly. 'Nobody's coming. You are all fakes. *Sab duplicate hai*!'

Victor spun around. 'Relax, Rahul. They should be here any minute.'

'You said that two hours ago!'

'Two hours? More like ten minutes.'

'*Chup*! Stop your *bakwas*!' His eyes blazed wildly, scanning the shed. They settled on a tawa leaning against the entrance wall. He lunged for it, grabbed and ran.

'That's our tawa for making pao-bhaji! We need it, Rahul! Stop!'

But Rahul's feet had found wings after a long time. He ran past the shanties, past the tap, to be arrested in his tracks by the same woman. 'Why are you running with a tawa, beta?' she asked gently. He hesitated, eyes softening. Then he heard footsteps behind. Slamming the tawa against the woman, he pushed her away and ran. But Victor grabbed the collar of Rahul's shirt. In the scuffle, the tawa rolled away. The inevitable crowd gathered.

'Thief! He's a thief!' cried an excited voice.

'Leave him alone,' panted Victor. 'The tawa is ours.'

'What about the woman. He hit her.'

Victor turned to the woman. 'Forgive him, ma-ji. He's not in his senses.'

She kept observing Rahul sadly. 'Anyone can see that.'

Though he was bathed and spruced up, Aparna was shocked at Rahul's appearance. He had grown tall but was as thin as a matchstick, arms covered with prickly red spots, bandy legs sticking out of shorts flapping effeminately around his thighs. His face was haggard, the cheeks hollow, but the amber eyes popping out of sunken sockets blazed raw passion.

'Why have you come so late!' he barked, glaring.

She ignored him. 'See who's come to see you,' she said as Bablu stepped into the shed.

'Where have you been all these months, yaar,' said Bablu, approaching him with both palms raised for a clasp. 'I've made kheer for you,' he said, thrusting a small steel box at his friend.

Rahul backed off, pushing it away. 'I don't want kheer! I want to leave. You can't keep me here. It's not a jail!'

Aparna saw he was in no state to connect. Fumbling in her handbag she brought out a strip of tablets and handed them to Shekhar. 'Give him one,' she instructed.

'Eat a little kheer first,' said Victor, opening Bablu's box.

Rahul flung the box against the wall, glaring at them

like a wild animal. Kheer splattered over the floor. '*Mader chod*! *Mujhe chhod*!' he snarled.

'Okay Rahul. Go,' said Aparna sternly. 'Don't stop him boys. If he wants to destroy himself no one can stop him.'

'In this state he could do anything, didi.'

She ignored Victor and turned to Rahul. 'Where will you go, Rahul?'

'Anywhere.'

'Wherever you can get your fix, right?' He looked sullen. 'You need it bad, don't you?' He remained silent. 'Do you have money, Rahul? How will you buy garda without money?'

It was as if she had touched a live wire. Anger energized his frail body, making it shiver and sweat at the same time. 'I have money!' he shouted. 'Thousands and thousands of rupees. A *mawali* stole it but I'm going to get it back.'

Victor and Aparna exchanged glances. 'Who's this *mawali*, Rahul? Maybe we can help you get your money back.'

'You are as bad as him! You won't give it to me.'

'Is he on drugs like you?'

'Mind your own business.'

'Is he?'

'No.'

'So let's try getting your money from him. You can't buy anything without money.'

'I'll get my money. I'll beat him, thrash him, kill him!' His voice had risen to a crescendo. Eyes spewed venom over them all. Blazing, they came to rest on Bablu. 'You! You know him!' he stormed, tapping two aggressive fingers on Bablu's chest.

Bablu backed off, hiding behind Victor. 'I? How do I know who?'

'Karim-bhai!'

'Karim-bhai? The fruit seller?'

'That's the one! He's a thief!'

'How?'

Aparna intervened again. 'That's not important at this juncture. The point is that Rahul needs his fix, needs money for his fix. How is he going to get it?' She looked Rahul squarely in the face. 'Are you serious about thrashing Karim-bhai?'

'Yes,' he said defiantly.

'Okay, go. We have nothing more to do with you.'

Suddenly he dropped on the chair, banging his head against the tin wall, painful moans escaping his lips. It was Shekhar's turn to intervene. He had crushed and dissolved the tablets in water. 'Just drink this, Rahul,' he said gently. 'Once you feel better we can talk.'

Trembling hands grasped the glass. A gulp downed water. He gagged, sputtered, coughed and sat down holding his head as spittle trickled off his chin. Temporarily, anger ebbed. Before the tide turned, Shekhar crushed another tablet. In half an hour he had drifted into sleep as they conferred outside the shed, hurling an avalanche of questions at Bablu. Did Rahul really have so much money? Who was Karim-bhai? Was he the type to steal?

'No, yaar. He's a nice guy. He used to give Rahul fruit for that baby. Remember Kajol? How he went crazy over her?'

'It's all because of that kid,' said Victor bitterly. 'If he hadn't got so involved he'd have stayed normal like us.'

'Don't blame the baby. Rahul's always been restless,' chided Aparna. 'Anyway, our immediate problem is where to keep him. Obviously he can't stay here.'

'Why not Sharan?' asked Bablu.

'Other boys are at risk.' She paused, reflecting. 'Did he really have so much money?' she asked Bablu incredulously.

He shrugged. 'He used to spend a lot. One day he said he was saving to buy a taxi.'

'Buy a taxi!'

'That's what he said. When I laughed he got angry and stopped meeting me.'

Aparna sighed, running a hand through her hair in disbelief. 'We have to meet this Karim-bhai. Do you know his stall?'

'It's been shut for two months.'

Aparna cut in. 'He may have gone to his village.'

'When he goes to his village his brother's son runs the shop. Just now it's all tied up with ropes.'

'Make inquiries. Boys, let Shekhar and me tackle Rahul alone when he wakes up. Go back to your work.'

Fuzzy contours. Patches of light and dark greys. Huddled forms murmuring. Rahul turned to the wall. Bones of stone, not lead. He bent his toes into curled knots. Knuckles cracked. The sound made him smile, a smirk seen only by the wavy wall. Grey. He curled his toes again. No crackle. The smile faded. Rahul turned flat on his back on the narrow bench and stared at the ceiling. More waves, more greys. Trapping heat indoors. Sweat clogging pores.

Aparna saw he was awake but didn't want to make the first move. Yet it was imperative to penetrate his fog before the sedative wore off. Deliberately she dropped a thali and watched it rotate noisily on the ground. The clattering made him sit up, eyes wide. She picked up the thali, returning it to the crockery stand. He examined her warily.

The previous exchange was a haze. Unconnected with the present.

'When did you come?' he asked.

'I've been waiting for you to wake up, Rahul,' she said, relaxing. 'You've stayed away for ages.'

His face crumpled like a ball of squashed newspaper. 'I . . . I should have stayed in touch, didi. *Bada bhool hua.*'

'Mistakes can be corrected, Rahul. How thin you've become! And you were all set to be such a success!'

His eyes brimmed. '*Poora sapna toot gaya.*'

'There are always setbacks, Rahul, but that doesn't mean one should lose sight of one's goals. The first thing is to get you well again. Then your dreams can come alive again. How long have you been on drugs?' He turned his palms upwards to indicate that he wasn't sure. 'Brown sugar, right?' He nodded. 'Chasing or injecting?'

'Both.'

'Have you been sharing needles with your friends?'

'Sometimes.'

'Don't you know the risk of HIV?'

He threw back his head defiantly. 'Everyone has to die.'

'Not at fourteen. Have you thought about what you'll do if you get AIDS?'

'Jump into the sea and drown. *Mere aage-peechhay koi nahin.*'

'If no one cared about you would Victor and Shekhar have come running? Would they have put aside everything to be with you?'

He raised his eyes to her face. Felt her concern. A tear escaped the corner of his eye. 'I'm not worth it, didi. I'm shit. Just *kuchra* . . .'

'Right now you are a mess. But you don't have to stay

that way. Lots of people get in and out of trouble. Don't you want to straighten out?'

His gaze dropped to the floor uncomfortably. 'I can't. I'm too far gone.'

'You were full of dreams. Don't you remember?'

'That was another life.'

'Tell me your last dream.' He shrugged, helplessly. 'Think, Rahul.'

He struggled with layers of images. Andy and Goa. Money, money, money. Always funny . . . Red dupatta in the sky . . . Chandni . . . Kajol in New York? Karen? Karim-bhai . . . Black tracks . . . black between tracks . . . black-and-yellow taxi . . . Yes-yes, taxi . . .

'I wanted to become a taxi driver,' he said brokenly.

'Becoming a taxi driver is not an empty dream like becoming a film star, Rahul,' said Aparna approvingly. 'You can do it. Once you are eighteen you can get a licence and learn to drive. But first you have to get well.'

He was looking at her with an incredulous expression. 'I . . .? Taxi driver?'

'Yes, when you're old enough.'

'But Karim-bhai has taken my money.'

'We'll find Karim-bhai. First we have to get you off drugs. Do you want to get off drugs?'

His face crumpled again. 'I . . . I can't.'

'On your own you can't. But now you're not alone. You are with friends. We can admit you to a detox centre where you'll be treated.'

'Will it be painful?'

Aparna minced no words. 'Yes, it will be painful. But you won't be alone. You'll be in a room with other boys going through the same treatment. It won't be easy. But it will take you back to your dream, closer to making the dream a reality. Once you are cured we can trace Karimbhai, make him return your money. When you turn eighteen you can go to a driving school, get your licence. Can you see Rahul driving on the streets of Bombay taking important people to Malabar Hill, Gateway of India . . .'

It was as if she had flung a lighted match on to a stack of dry grass.

'No!' he shouted. 'No Gateway of India! Dirty place. Dirty, dirty . . .'

The delirium was coming on. Aparna signalled to Shekhar for another tablet. As Rahul's eyes glazed he kept muttering, 'Dirty . . . dirty place . . .' She fed him what remained of Bablu's kheer, followed by the tablet. He slept like a baby.

nineteen

H e was tense, sitting awkwardly on an overturned wooden crate outside Sharan. Victor was late. The waiting was gnawing at his innards. He longed for a drag to help him relax. To banish the thought, he examined the chappals on his feet. They were slightly big for him, but new; rubber *do-patti*s in an unusual shade of red, gifted by Aparna when he was discharged from the detox centre after five horrendous days. His prize for coming through.

Being barefoot hadn't bothered him as a child. He got his first pair of chappals when he started visiting Kajol in hospital. At Bal Kendra he was given chappals with his clothes and at the Gateway there was always an assortment of discarded footwear left behind by travellers. Often battered, sometimes not. But after Dinesh sold a pair of Reeboks for three hundred rupees Rahul realized that shoes have a value beyond protecting soles. One by one the shoes went in the daily demand for a fix.

Wearing chappals, however cheap, made him feel well-heeled again, like a savage returning to civilization. He wriggled his toes, catching sunlight on the straps. The third toe of his left foot had a crescent-shaped scab. He couldn't remember how or where he had hurt his foot. It didn't hurt any longer. The wound on his cheek had healed, leaving a pink welt. The scar would fade with time. His cheeks were beginning to fill out. His body, which had shrivelled to skin and bones, was regaining flesh, the amber eyes their lustre.

For a month he had been living at Sharan, sleeping the better part of the day, strolling through the flower market or the fruit market, thinking of Chandni, depressed to find Karim-bhai's stall shut. Most things were as they used to be, including Hamid's stall. But Rahul had changed. He no longer coveted shirts. He had no interest in filching fruit.

A telephone booth run by handicapped persons had come up on the opposite pavement. Every morning a young woman would weave her way through the traffic on a hand-operated tricycle. She was paraplegic below the waist but cheerfully chatted and joked with Sharan's boys. Aparna pointed her out as an example of courage in adversity.

'Everyone gets on with life despite problems,' she told Rahul. 'Sumangali has to live with her ungainly body but see how well she goes about it.'

He watched Sumangali from across the street, admiring the way she steered her strange cycle in traffic. But Aparna's moralizing irritated him.

This was a crucial day. He and Victor were going to look for Karim-bhai. Uncertain whether they would find him, unsure what to say if they did. Rahul hadn't kept accounts or taken receipts. He couldn't even remember how much he had saved, just that it was a lot. His anxiety increased.

Aparna's attitude indicated she didn't quite believe him. 'If you've earned so much, you can earn it again,' she said, trying to dissuade him from following up on Karim-bhai. 'Don't risk a relapse by running into the arms of disappointment.' For all she did, her advice depressed him.

Rahul knew he would never earn big money as long as he stayed at Sharan. The Gateway offered an enchanted life that attracted him despite all the upheavals. He had decided to return to the tourist trade. Without garda he would be in control again. He would differentiate between the Andys and the Gregs. He had experience. He would stay away from danger. He would save for his taxi, even if it meant starting from scratch. He just had to get strong again. He needed his Sharan friends to get his money back. Then he would leave.

Hesitantly he crossed over to the telephone booth. 'Hello,' he said shyly, peering in. He was approaching a stranger for the first time since his recovery.

Sumangali looked up from the recipe pages of *Chitralekha* magazine. 'Hello. You're new at Sharan?'

He smiled wryly. 'I used to live here long ago. There was no telephone booth then.'

'It's been here nearly two years.'

'I've been away a long time.'

'Did you go back to your family?'

'I have no family. I only have Sharan.'

She looked at him quizzically. 'It's quite a unique place, isn't it? Boys come, boys go. Those who leave invariably come back.'

He didn't want to talk about Sharan so he asked, 'Have you been here for two years?'

'A blind boy was here before me. Now he has a job in an office.'

'Will you also get a job in an office?'

A shadow crossed her face. 'Only if they find a special kind of employer. Jobs are difficult to find. A receptionist doesn't only have to be good at her work. She has to be pretty.'

He didn't know what to say. 'But you are so . . .'

'Pretty? I'm not. But I'm lucky. I have a good husband even if he's blind. And a child in school. Don't feel sorry for me.'

He smiled widely. 'I was going to say you are so brave.'

She laughed, a light tinkling laugh he didn't expect from a person with an ugly body. 'God works in strange ways,' she said. 'Takes away something, gives something else. You never know what challenge he's going to throw at you next.'

Rahul was in no mood to think about god. Relieved to see Victor striding up, he moved away. As a mere formality they walked to the boarded-up fruit stall. Bablu had been talking to neighbouring hawkers and had found out that Karim-bhai had turned strange after the Gujarat riots. He was no longer the cheerful person people had known. It was rumoured he had lost his family in the riots. One day they found the fruit stall boarded up with no sign of Karim-bhai. They suspected he had joined an extremist group.

Bablu was unconvinced. 'He's a nice man, yaar. We must find him,' he kept saying.

Rahul had no difficulty locating the barsati. Nothing had changed except the faces. New occupants, younger, but just as decrepit. Karim-bhai's bed still had the stained mosquito net, with fresh patches covering holes. It was occupied by a sardar. The new attendant couldn't recall Karim-bhai. Disappointed, Rahul was turning away when he spotted Girish the tailor pedalling away with the pencil stub poised behind his ear as before.

'Namaste, Girish-bhai,' he began tentatively.

The tailor squinted at him behind thick glasses. 'You-ou-ou! You are the one who made a mess of my curtains, right?'

Guiltily Rahul covered his mouth. 'I delivered them . . .'

'And almost lost me one of my biggest clients! Girish forgets nothing. I don't see very well but my brain stores every detail.' He took off his spectacles, stopping work. 'Eh, *chhokra*,' he called to a boy standing near the stairs. '*Teen chai lao. Jaldi.*'

'Don't bother, chacha. We don't want tea.'

Girish dismissed the objection with a swish of his wrist. 'Have you come to book a bed again?'

'We've come looking for Karim-bhai.'

Girish shut his eyes, heaving a deep sigh. 'Poor man. He's gone.'

'Gone?'

'Back to the village to die. He has cancer.'

'No!'

'He was in great pain. His wife came to Bombay. Took him to doctors, hospitals. No use.' Noticing Rahul's face he asked, 'What's the matter?'

'I . . . I was very fond of him.'

'He used to talk about you, seemed worried you'd got into bad company. Before leaving Bombay he kept saying he wished he knew where you were.'

Rahul bit his lip as a dry sob escaped. Victor came to his rescue. 'Did Karim-bhai leave anything for Rahul?' he asked. 'Any message?'

The tea arrived in small steel *vatki*s, covered by smaller *vatki*s to keep it hot. Girish passed them around, waving away the boy with a ten-rupee note.

'Message? I don't think so. But he did leave an address. The new fellow's a lazy bugger. Won't give you a thing without a tip.'

Sure enough, the surly attendant had a memory flash when a five-rupee coin appeared. He pulled out old diaries, ran a finger down pages and finally scribbled an address on the back of a grocery bill. Someone called Yusuf Sheikh living in Kurla.

Rahul's head was spinning. Karim-bhai's impending death as traumatic as the receding prospects of recovering his money. He desperately needed a joint. Desperately needed to deny death, betrayal. Desperately needed to flee.

Victor caught his arm. 'We're going to Kurla,' he said.

'Kurla? Why?'

'To meet Yusuf Sheikh. Find out whether Karim-bhai is alive, where he is.'

'Girish said he's gone to his village.'

'Which village? Where?'

'What use is that?'

'We've come so far, we have to follow up,' said Victor. He was reluctant to leave Rahul in a limbo, afraid the unstable boy would fall prey to his poison yet again.

The speed and the crowds on the train unnerved Rahul. Victor kept a protective arm around him as they straphung, standing for the first two stops, and ushered him to the first seat vacated by a fat man. The man has a hot bum, thought Rahul mischievously as warmth permeated his pants. But when they got off at Kurla he was shivering.

Victor led him to the tea stall. The overly sweet tea

gagged his throat. He sat on a bench, head between palms, staring at rail tracks. Fixed from point to point, allowing no change of direction. Fixed as the moon in the sky, changing shape, remaining unchanged. Fixed as the lines on his palm.

Under a distant overbridge he spotted the huddle of boys. One after the other they leaned towards a flame. He could almost sense the inhalation of bitter smoke into lungs. His yearning intensified. How to escape Victor? But Victor had followed Rahul's gaze. Very firmly he led Rahul out of the station and hustled him into an auto, showing the driver the address.

It was a dilapidated single-storeyed building propped up on bamboos. The staircase was liberally stained with splashes of paan. The board on the first landing read 'Yusuf Sheikh, Advocate'. Three clients were in the reception room. Rahul drummed his fingers on his knee, nervous and impatient. He was ready to give up the wild goose chase, his longing to join the boys escaping into bliss becoming stronger as the minutes passed. But there was no escaping Victor.

At last they were in Yusuf Sheikh's cabin. He was bearded, like Karim-bhai, but capless. His first question was, 'How do I know you are the same Rahul? I need proof.'

They were nonplussed. 'I am Rahul. Karim-bhai's friend. Ask him.'

'That's not possible. That's why I need proof. Someone to vouch for you. Sign an affidavit.'

'Why? We just want to find Karim-bhai.'

'He has passed away. But I have an envelope for a fourteen- or fifteen-year-old boy called Rahul. If you are the same boy, prove it.'

They left in a daze. Had Karim-bhai left the money in an envelope? A cheque perhaps? What a cat-and-mouse game they had got into! How on earth was he to prove he was he?

It turned out to be easier than anticipated. Aparna wrote a letter on Sharan's letterhead identifying Rahul. Yusuf Sheikh examined it, made a couple of calls, then solemnly handed Rahul a large brown envelope.

'Karim was a distant relative,' he said mistily. 'He was very fond of you, beta. Never forget that.'

The envelope was bulky but it didn't feel like money. Rahul could feel no currency notes as he turned it over in his hand. Victor had observed Rahul's roving eye, the hands that kept pinching clothes in nervous tension, the tremors coursing through his body. He insisted they reach Sharan before opening the envelope. The return ride was agony as curiosity and impatience battled against caution. As soon as they reached Sharan Rahul tore open the envelope and pulled out a document and a long hand-written letter. No money, no cheque, no bank books. His heart sank. His money was gone. He was sure of that now. Aparna's scepticism would give way to disbelief. She might even dismiss his experiences as fantasy. That would be salt on a raw wound.

As soon as she arrived they settled into a corner away from other boys, and she began to read.

My dear bachcha,

I don't know if this letter will reach you, or whether I'll be in this world when it does. The less we remember our last meeting the better. I would rather not see you again than see you in such a state. But something tells me you will recover and come searching for me.

By the time you get this you will have heard about my cancer. It is a painful illness, but I am not sorry to die. I have been afflicted by another kind of pain for a long, long time. The pain of watching the world change in front of my eyes, of watching evil grow more and more powerful. Dying will end the pain of being a helpless spectator.

After my sister's death I was plagued with thoughts of revenge. One rapist is known to me. Many nights I'd stay awake planning to find him, confront him, kill him. I didn't care if I was killed as well. Only one thought obsessed me: to teach him a lesson.

If I didn't act, it was for only one reason—my son. How will my son face the world if his father becomes a murderer? What kind of man will he grow up to be? Is a legacy of revenge all I can leave him? What kind of father will I be if I leave him infected with the virus of hatred?

These people were insane when they did what they did. No one in their right senses rapes and kills. When sanity returns will they be ashamed? Will they be afraid of people like me? The fact that they deny what they did means they know it is wrong. But instead of asking forgiveness of God they band together in mass denial. As if the devil has taken possession of their senses!

Bachcha, ours has been a strange and special bond. You are almost the same age as my son. I have watched you grow from innocence to depravity. I have seen you struggle to make something of your life. Failure doesn't reveal the intensity of struggle, especially when the odds are against you.

Since the day you threatened me with a knife I have been praying for you; don't ask me why. I have stopped

*believing in God. What kind of God allows women to be
raped and murdered? What kind of God allows criminals
to go scot-free? What kind of God allows a motherless,
fatherless child to grow up in the streets and then drives
him mad? Is this God blind? Deaf? Weak? Has he sold
out to the devil?*

*I have no faith in today's God. Yet I pray out of habit
and helplessness. Because I don't know what else to do. If
by some miracle you recover, my prayers will have been
answered, whether I live to see it or not.*

*Your money has been on my conscience. I often
wondered what to do with it. If I knew where your mother
and sisters are I would have sent it to them. I am convinced
I was right in not giving it to you when you were half
mad.*

*Then illness struck. Medicines are expensive. Your money
was lying unused. Temptation grew strong. Forgive me,
bachcha, in the weakness of pain I used your money for
my treatment. But I have tried to make up. I have made
over my fruit stall to you. Yusuf Sheikh will take care of
the formalities. He will make the licence in your name. He
will give you a loan to start. When you recover you will
have an honest profession waiting . . .*

Aparna's voice broke off as soft sobs punctuated the
quiet. Rahul's nails were digging into Victor's forearm. Victor
ran his free hand over steamy eyes. Then the moment passed.

A whirlwind raged through Rahul's head. Past and future
imploding. Making the present tenuous. Emotions.
Recriminations. Decisions. Fear of losing friends. Fear of
being alone again combined with the certainty that alone
is what he had to be.

A long time passed before Aparna asked, 'Is running a fruit stall what you want to do?'

He kept looking into space blankly. She repeated her question. He remained mute.

Then Bablu said, 'You wanted to start a banana business, remember?'

'That was before . . .'

'Before what?'

He looked from one face to another, his face devoid of expression. 'Before I learnt to live,' he said simply.

'What do you mean by "live"? That depraved life has taken you down the drain,' retorted Aparna sharply.

He shook his head. 'No. I made money. I ate in hotels. I got gifts. I went inside Taj.'

'What are you saying? You suffered, you were on drugs, you came to us half dead. You could have got AIDS and died!'

'I don't care if I die. But if I live I want to live well.'

'Live well! You were still *sadak chhaap*.'

'I was *sadak chhaap* with Denim aftershave.'

'Denim aftershave? Where did you get aftershave?'

'Friends.'

'Which friends?'

'Foreigners. Coming-going, having fun.'

'Fun with foreigners?'

He looked at her candidly, aware he was going to shock. But this was no time for soft-pedalling. He had to speak out. Because his decision was final, not subject to her approval.

'Massage,' he said, as gently as he could.

Aparna blinked. 'Massage?' she asked, not registering. But Victor's and Shekhar's eyes widened.

'Getting money for massaging foreigners,' he said, meeting her eye.

Aparna's hand rose to her mouth, unconsciously crushing Karim-bhai's letter. Her head swam. She struggled to compose a mask over rioting thoughts.

'You made money massaging foreigners in hotel rooms?' she asked, not succeeding in keeping her voice even. His eyes pleaded understanding. 'And you want to go back to that?' Without flinching he nodded. Her mouth dropped. 'Why?' she asked, barely audible.

'Better than station life.'

'Better than being among friends?'

'I had other friends.'

'Where were they when you were in trouble?'

'Trouble comes, trouble goes. Who doesn't have troubles?'

'You're only fourteen, Rahul, but you've been through a lot. You can tell the difference between true friends and fair-weather friends.'

He looked at her in a way that made her squirm. 'You are born alone, you die alone. In between people come and go.'

He was too cynical for his age, she thought. That deepened her dilemma. She was trained to respect children's choices. But that was in the context of family, education, employment. Nothing had prepared her to accept a child's decision to return to prostitution. Looking at the crumpled paper in dismay she unclenched her fist and tried to straighten Karim-bhai's letter. But the creases remained.

'Let's talk about it tomorrow, Rahul. We've had a long day,' she said, bargaining for time.

But Rahul's life had no space for her dilemmas. He had decided to go his own way.

twenty

A heady taste of salt made Rahul's nostrils tingle as he drew air deeply into his lungs. One breath after another coursed life into his veins. His chest swelled and his muscles relaxed as sea air swirled inwards, cleansing him. His eyes settled on gently sloping mountains connected by a flat strip, the clear air making buildings visible on the distant shore. The sun's reflection on water increased the late morning glare. Rahul revelled at the expanse of unlimited sky, marvelled at the tenacity of pigeons pecking pavement cracks for grain, smiled at the pop of a child's heart-shaped balloon. The familiarity of the boatmen's quarrelling voices told him he was home. Peering over the ledge he tried to follow the fight. They were on the decks of two boats, tethered to an in-between boat with ropes. Both dark-skinned, with lungis drawn up above their knees, barking abuses in a language he didn't understand. He liked their waggling arms, flashing teeth, threatening postures rendered safe by distance. Daily quarrels, as predictable as sunrise.

Rahul lingered on the pier, staring at the equestrian statue of the Maratha warrior, Shivaji. A formidable leader, but no role model for Rahul. He had no ambition to raise an army, fight wars, rule a kingdom. Strange that Victor,

Shekhar and others had considered him, Rahul, their role model! Based on illusions. Even stranger, that their affection remained, despite disillusion.

They had spent days trying to talk him out of returning to the Gateway, taking the role of the elder brothers he never had. Half-heartedly he tried to fit into the life they suggested, working at the pao-bhaji stall, chatting with Sumangali who knew nothing about the darker side of his life, being counselled, endlessly counselled, by Aparna. Not satisfied with counselling she even took him to meet a lawyer called Thomas. He couldn't fathom why.

'We must put an end to these lecherous men corrupting our kids,' she said.

The lawyer seemed as charged up. He asked Rahul about the nationalities of the men he had been with, the hotels they frequented, the rates they paid. Then the more intimate questions. What exactly they did, what they asked him to do, whether he was forced into acts he didn't want. Rahul answered sullenly, only half truthful. Much as he would have liked to get the law after Greg, he had nothing against the likes of Andy.

'Have you been taken to Goa?' asked Thomas.

The question caught him off guard. 'Next year,' he said without thinking.

'With who?'

'Andy.'

'Who's Andy?'

Rahul held a sullen silence.

'Where's he from?'

'America.'

'Where in America?'

He looked at Thomas warily. 'Why do you want to know?'

'To trace him. Paedophiles shouldn't be allowed to roam around the world freely.'

Alarm bells went off in Rahul's head. Andy was his friend. They had good times together. He didn't want to get Andy into trouble.

'What does this Andy look like?' the lawyer continued.

'Dark, with a long nose and spectacles,' lied Rahul.

'Do you have a photograph?'

'No.'

'Did Andy take photographs?'

He hesitated. 'Greg did,' he replied to deflect attention.

'Who's Greg?'

Rahul's lower lip quivered as memories of that horrendous night surfaced. He broke into shivers, sweaty palms leaving smudges on the lawyer's polished table. Thomas and Aparna watched Rahul's face contort, his knuckles turn pale, his eyes become glazed, unseeing.

'Who is Greg?' asked Aparna gently. 'Did he hurt you?'

What could he say? Maybe to Victor, or Shekhar. But Aparna . . . and a stranger? He drew in his breath for self-control.

'I can see you've had a bad experience,' coaxed Aparna. 'If you tell us we can help you, Rahul.'

A dry sob escaped his quivering lips as his mouth twisted into an expression of disgust. Looking down at taut knuckles he whispered, 'Made me bleed.'

'They . . .? Bleed? Where?'

Again Rahul struggled to find words. Slowly he lifted his left hand and pointed to his buttocks. Aparna gasped.

'Greg sodomized you,' said Thomas matter-of-factly.

'Did you see a doctor?' Rahul shook his head. 'Damn! Why didn't you see a doctor? We need evidence!'

'That's enough, Thomas! Can't you see the child is traumatized?'

'Sorry,' retreated Thomas, jotting furiously on his notepad. 'Can you describe this Greg?'

'He had long hair . . . tied at the back . . . earring . . . gold in his teeth . . .' began Rahul haltingly. 'And he had an Indian friend who spoke foreign language.'

'Which language?' Rahul shrugged. 'Where did you meet them?'

'Apollo. We went to Baghdadi. Then to Narain's house.'

'Narain's house!' exclaimed Thomas and Aparna together. 'Who's Narain?'

'Greg's friend. Lives in a big bungalow with chains inside. No people. No one can hear shouting.'

'Can you take us to this house?'

'*Kabhi nahin*!'

Aparna put an arm on his shoulder. He wrenched away as if stung. 'No! Never to that house again!' he shuddered. Pushing his chair back, he retreated, hitting the cabin door, and fled without looking back. He headed neither for Sharan nor for Victor's and Shekhar's shack but went straight to a paan-wallah, bought a *goli* and sat on the dry grass of a maidan rolling his joint. An overpowering need to soothe raw nerves engulfed him. Inhaling loosened the knots in his stomach. But he didn't let himself fly. Once the trauma of terrifying memories abated, he stubbed out the joint, put what was left of it into his shirt pocket and allowed calm thoughts to settle in his head.

For once Aparna seemed to be on the right track. People like Greg and Narain deserved to be put in their place. But they seemed to be gunning for Andy as well. He had no grudge against Andy. Should he cooperate? Would he be able to find Narain's house? What would they do if he took them there?

Shekhar confronted him the day after his meeting with Thomas. 'You must consult a doctor,' he said coming to the point. 'There's risk of HIV.'

Rahul kept his eyes on the crescent-shaped mark on his toe. The scab had dropped off, revealing soft pink flesh. He still passed blood with his stool. And it was painful. He had told no one about it. Doctors were terrors anyway.

'I still bleed every day, Shekhar,' he said softly. 'And it's painful. Sleeping or standing is okay, but sitting . . .'

Shekhar's face hardened. 'Are you mad that you still want to go back to that dirty life?' he exploded, banging a palm against his forehead.

'The pain's not as bad as it used to be,' Rahul said defensively. 'Okay, I'll go to a doctor if you want, but we know what doctors are like.'

Aparna arranged for him to see a private doctor who took blood and urine samples, then examined him behind a green cloth screen while she waited in the ante-room.

'The rectal muscles have prolapsed,' he told Aparna, removing the rubber gloves and washing his hands while Rahul dressed. 'He needs surgery. He'll have to be admitted to hospital.'

Rahul was apprehensive but with Aparna in charge he knew he was in good hands. And he had to get fit before returning to the Gateway. The yearning for drugs was under control but another kind of yearning took over. His body made demands as insistent as Venkat's. The *hath-gadi* technique brought relief but little pleasure. For fun you needed a partner. For partners he needed Apollo Bunder. Two years of active sex made him hungry for more.

Aparna would never reconcile with his decision any more than he could lead the life she wanted. She was too much of a prude to risk pain for pleasure. In two years he had experienced more than she would in a lifetime. Which disqualified her as counsellor.

'Have you thought of all the implications of what you want, Rahul?' she would say in a self-righteous tone that got on his nerves.

'Yes, didi,' he would reply for the umpteenth time. 'I want money. I want fun. I want to have a good life.'

'That's fine at fourteen. You know these men only want kids. What'll you do when you're twenty-five?'

'I'll be a taxi driver.'

'So run the fruit stall till you're eighteen. Or take up a job. Would you like to learn motor mechanics? That will help you maintain your taxi.' He agreed to give it a try.

She apprenticed him to Pingle's garage at the end of a dead-end lane where six cars were parked in a stamp-sized space. Neither Pingle nor his assistants had time to teach a novice. Rahul was told to watch and learn. He hung around for seven days doing nothing more exciting than passing tools to heads under bonnets. On the eighth day he quit.

One hot afternoon, a month after his surgery, he took the plunge, approaching Victor's stall with Karim-bhai's letter in his pocket. Despite the heavy lunch-hour crowd Victor thrust a plate of pao-bhaji into his hands. Rahul pushed it away.

'I've come to talk business,' he said abruptly. 'Do you want Karim-bhai's stall?'

Victor continued to soak paos in hot butter on the tawa. 'Why don't you try running it? We can help,' he said at last.

'I've had enough. I'm well now. I have to leave.'

'Come and stay with us. Try the fruit business. The Gateway won't run away.' He put the butter-soaked pao on a thali beside the spicy, aromatic bhaji and handed it to a client.

Rahul sighed in exasperation. Living with Victor and Shekhar wouldn't work. Already he found them overbearing. Sooner or later he would have to escape. That would damage their friendship. Turning to Victor he asked candidly, 'How much would I earn?'

'Twelve, maybe fifteen thousand.'

'When Andy comes we spend that in two-three days.'

Victor's blood boiled to hear Rahul speak so casually of his depraved life. 'What if Andy doesn't return?' he asked, gritting his teeth.

'There'll be others.'

'Aren't you ashamed to talk like this?' he exclaimed, unable to hide his disgust.

'Don't start like didi,' pleaded Rahul wearily. 'I'm getting paid for performing a service. Tell me, do you or do you not want the stall?'

Victor wiped perspiration from his forehead and flicked it to the ground. 'I have to talk to Anand,' he muttered. 'We'll let you know.'

Rahul was not prepared for Thomas turning up at Sharan late one evening. 'Come to my car so we can talk privately,' said Thomas briskly when Sharan's younger boys stared. They had followed Aparna's order to keep a distance from Rahul. But a sahab who came in a car was too much.

'Aparna tells me you want to return to Apollo Bunder,' began Thomas, switching off the ignition at a quiet corner near Shivaji Park where couples strolled among lengthening shadows, lost in each other's dreams. 'I've been telling her to accept your decision. Society does little enough for kids like you. We have no right to stop you from taking your life into your own hands.'

Rahul's brow puckered. If Thomas meant what he said then why was he here?

'Rahul knows I think differently,' cut in Aparna, turning around to face Rahul in the back seat. 'We'll do anything to help you straighten out.'

'Your idea of straighten out means conforming and Rahul doesn't want to conform,' responded Thomas. Turning to Rahul he continued, 'Even when you go your own way you have to take care of yourself, right Rahul? You have to make sure these dirty men play straight with you, right?'

Rahul nodded cautiously, his suspicions fully aroused.

'Did you know what you were getting into when you went to that house with Greg and his friend?'

'No.'

'If you'd known would you have gone?'

'Never!'

'You told us Greg took photographs, right? What kind of photos?'

How was he to answer that? 'Photo . . . like playing with . . .'

'Pornographic photographs?'

'Meaning?'

'Photographs of people having sex?'

'Some. Also with toys, clothes . . .'

'Toys?'

Involuntarily he giggled. 'You know . . . golden hair . . . ladies' socks . . . make-up. . .'

'And you enjoyed taking those photos, Rahul?'

He giggled again.

'Did you see the photographs?'

'On camera only.'

'Do you know what Greg does with such photographs?'

'Not Greg. Photos with Andy.' The gaffe hit him only after he had spoken. But there was no way to backtrack. 'Andy was fun,' he said defiantly.

'But not Greg?'

'No.'

'Do you know what people like Greg and Andy do with such photographs, Rahul?' He hadn't thought of that. 'They sell them for thousands of rupees. Did they pay you for the photos?'

Andy had given him lots of money when he left. Was that a gift or payment? This Thomas was too wily. Rahul didn't like him.

'Instead of cross-examining Rahul, tell him your plan,' intervened Aparna, smiling at the worried-looking boy. 'Don't be afraid, Rahul. No one will know if you help us. And if ever you have a bad experience we'll be there to help you.'

Thomas changed tack, switching to a more cajoling tone. 'Men like Greg, Andy and others are part of an international pornographic racket. Not only do they ruin the lives of small children, they also sell your pictures for thousands of dollars. That's how they are able to travel, spend, travel, spend. And children like you become their victims.'

He didn't see himself as a victim of photography. Only sadism. Privately he resolved to charge a fee in future. But what did Thomas want him to do?

'My colleagues and I have been tracking this racket for months,' continued Thomas. 'Groups of people who have sex with children and sell vulgar photographs have been active in Goa, Sri Lanka, Nepal, Rajasthan. For years they used to go to Thailand to satisfy their lust but since the Thai government has taken an active role to protect their children, sex tourists have started coming to India. We're trying to make our government take notice of what's going on. For that we need your cooperation.'

Rahul examined Thomas's face as warily as he would a cobra's. The soft hiss before the sting? Why didn't he come to the point?

'We'll take you for a drive, Rahul,' continued Thomas. 'Just guide us to Narain's house. You don't have to get out of the car. No one will know who took us there. We want to nab Narain and Greg so that no other children suffer like you.'

Thomas made it sound disarmingly simple. But suppose he stopped at the house? Suppose the car got a puncture and they had to get out? Suppose Greg or Narain spotted him in the car?

Aparna seemed to have read his thoughts. 'We'll take you in a car with tinted glass, Rahul. No one will be able to look inside.'

He knew about cars with tinted glass. He and Bablu would press the faces to the windows of such cars at traffic lights, laughing at the people cowering inside. It would be a change to look at the world from inside one. But what price should he demand for the risk?

'Five hundred rupees,' he said suddenly, taking Thomas by surprise.

'Five hundred . . .? For what?'

'For showing you the house.'

Thomas grimaced. 'Mercenary kid,' he muttered under his breath.

'What do you need money for?' asked Aparna.

'Shirt, shoes, biryani . . .'

'Not drugs?'

'No.'

'Suppose we buy you a shirt and shoes and treat you to biryani?'

He considered that. He needed to be better dressed before returning to Apollo Bunder. And it was ages since he had eaten at Baghdadi.

A week later he was again in the back seat of Thomas's car, wearing brand new jeans and a T-shirt with Shah Rukh Khan winking cheekily at all who passed. A deal had been worked out. Victor and Anand would convert Karim-bhai's stall into a snacks stall. Bablu would join the business. Rahul would be paid in instalments deposited in a bank account. His goal was to save for a taxi in four years when he turned eighteen. Their role was to repay him while ensuring he didn't get too much money too soon. Aparna had gone along with the arrangement that enabled them to keep an eye on him. That was the best she could do. Rahul was pleased with the arrangement because it prevented him from becoming isolated again. It gave him confidence and lessened his need to fly.

Their first stop was Baghdadi. Rahul had insisted on

that. Thomas sat drumming his fingers on the ridge of the Formica table, watching Rahul eat with relish. Ignoring the spoon and fork, he used his fingers to mix the masalas thoroughly. Lifting a double-jointed leg of chicken by its bone he bit into the pungent flesh, eyes closed.

And opened them to a bald head. The man's back was towards them. His shoulders were slumped. He was waiting to be served. Rahul couldn't spot the wide-brimmed straw hat Narain usually carried, nor could he see the man's face, but his fingers froze. He kept examining the bald-headed figure, saw a waiter place a leg of tandoori chicken in front of it.

He would have to pass the table to reach the wash basin. And risk exposure. He waited till the head was occupied with the chicken, then stealthily crept past, gargled, spat the last remnants of spice into swirling water and headed for the cash counter where Thomas was paying the bill, keeping his back towards the bald head. He didn't want to know whether it was Narain. That would save him from having to tell Thomas.

They cruised past Cuffe Parade's high rises, tension mounting as Rahul recognized the sentry posts. Then his mind went blank. He could not remember whether the cab had turned left, right or gone straight, could not connect with any landmarks around. Thomas drove down a lane with rows of identical apartment blocks. It was unfamiliar. He drove down another road shaded by towering trees. Rahul was certain he had never been here before.

'I bet you're fibbing!' barked an exasperated Thomas. 'Leading us on a wild goose chase.'

Rahul stared blankly at his back. 'The drive was your idea, not Rahul's,' defended Aparna. 'We knew he might not remember.'

'We've kept our end of the deal. He should keep his.'

Rahul was glad he had not recognized the house. He did not want to help Thomas. Not even if he was treated to biryani for a week. After almost two hours of driving down every possible alley they dropped him at the Gateway, the lawyer gloomily grumbling that the breakthrough had been 'so near and yet so far'.

As he sauntered down the pier, smiling to himself, Rahul realized that the best part of returning to the Gateway was not having to make a break with his old and trusted friends. It gave security to his freedom. Blinking at the old familiarities he stretched his hands wide, raising them to the sky. With all its perils and frills, this is where he wanted to be. Taking his time he strolled amidst the waddling pigeons, spotting one with an injured wing, observing tourists, not yet accosting them. As always, seagulls soared, foam curled around the lighthouse, boats left a widening V in their wake. At the end of the pier he stopped, took a deep breath of clean, salty air. Emptied his lungs. Took another breath. Then he walked up to the Radio Club adda.